Ganges
Ghosts

Tales Of Shotley
Peninsula, Suffolk

Len Biddlecombe

BLACKHEATH DAWN
Publishing

Hafren House, Blackheath, Wenhaston.
Suffolk IP19 9HB
enquiries.blackheathdawn@gmail.com
© Len Biddlecombe 2017

ISBN 978-1-911368-090 (eBook)
978-1-911368-175 (Paperback)

Ganges Ghosts is a collection of tales and
local lore from the Shotley Peninsular,
Suffolk. It reflects the author's experiences
over time and the exercise of his imagination.
Some names/characters have been added or
altered to ensure pertinent dialogue
Any resemblance to anyone, living or dead is
entirely coincidental.
For more information and detail of other
books by Len Biddlecombe

Enquiries.Blackheathdawn@gmail.com

I dedicate this book to my dear father
Ike,
(1888-1972)

I am only sorry that he will not be able to read it, however it is fitting to dedicate this book to his memory as I know how much HMS Ganges meant to him and a tremendous amount of the facts forming the backbone to my story came from his memories of the many happy years that he served there.

Len Biddlecombe

To Sue

Thank you for buying "GG"

Ken Beattie

Ganges Ghosts.

HMS GANGES has a wonderful history spanning 74 long years sitting on the end of the Shotley peninsula. A shore base training establishment, responsible for training over 150,000 boy entrants in seamanship and preparing them for a career in the Royal Navy.

The whole population of the Shotley peninsula is particularly fond and even proud of their relationships with HMS Ganges.

Len Biddlecomb's experiences of the area and particularly the shore base, stem from living in the village of Shotley where as a boy he would delight in being invited to the annual Guy Fawkes celebrations and accompanying his father who became the printer at the base.
Len's own employment at the establishment began when he was involved with security of the Eurosport Village and later with the transformation to a training centre for Suffolk Constabulary.

The site became the objective of a proposed massive building project but eventually closed its doors in 2007.

The Ganges museum continues to support the memories, aspirations and heroics of those 150,000+ Ganges Boys who found comradeship and personal worth in Shotley.

Len's knowledge of the site together with his many experiences complements his easy story telling style, when he draws from the many eerie tales that abound in the area.

Ganges Ghosts.

Chapter 1.

A Burning Desire.

From the very first day of my life, 4th. November 1922 my burning desire was for a career in the Royal Navy. My father, Captain Robert Smith had served in the force for many years and had come through the First World War with distinction, commanding several different warships and surviving three sinkings at the hands of the German navy. Hostilities had ceased for three years when he was released from active service with the rank of Commodore. He took a shore job. I apparently appeared as a result of his return home and with this in mind it was hardly surprising that I should want to follow in his footsteps. With his advice and a considerable amount of his help I opted for a career in telecommunications. At the age of fifteen , August 1938,, I applied to leave school and was granted permission to take up a career in the Royal Navy, taking a fifteen-month course at one of the shore based training camps. This was to be followed by a period of specialist training, and then, on successfully completing my exams. I hoped to be accepted for a course in telecommunications. Probably thanks to my father's influence and his delight, I was offered a position at HMS GANGES, a shore based training establishment in Suffolk. I had never even heard of it but my father was over the moon for me. 'They'll make a man of you' he declared and, sure enough, I was to remember those words over the coming months. It was with some trepidation that I said goodbye to my mum and dad early on 30th September,1938,and set off for Liverpool Lime Street Station to commence my long, long journey to Suffolk.

For the first time in my life I left home and the comparative safety of my mother's company; she had become used to running the home single handed in my father's absence. With my rail pass in hand I boarded the Boat Train to Harwich Town, where I was to be met and then taken to Harwich Pier to continue my journey, by boat, across the river to Shotley.

I felt nervous, yet very proud. I, David

Smith was beginning the first day of my new life, determined to make my father proud of me, determined to make a success of my new career. I was cheered up considerably when three other lads about my age joined the train on its way across the country all heading for the same destination and all just as frightened as I was, certainly it helped a lot. We arrived at Harwich just before dark and as promised were met by a Naval Petty Officer to escort us on the short journey from the station to the pier where a navy motor boat was waiting for us.

The journey across Harwich Harbour took little more than ten minutes and we were soon being marched up a vast number of steps apparently called Faith, Hope and Charity, past the Wardroom, over the Quarterdeck to report to the Guardroom where our credentials were checked and we were allocated to our respective divisions. I was assigned to Grenville, Class 60 and we were informed our Commanding Officer was Captain Corson. I would receive one shilling and sixpence each week, pocket money, but any provisions or toiletries I required could be booked to me and would be deducted from my pay credits. On leaving HMS Ganges my remaining credits would be paid to me. Despite all the bad publicity I had heard about the place, I must confess I found Ganges a wonderful place to be once I settled in. It bred a sense of comradeship way above any I ever felt in my entire career. Many people felt it was a horrible place to train and we all hated something about each day but somehow we relied on each other's help in all sorts of ways till we came to respect each other and as any ex Ganges boy will tell you there will never be a place where friendships were cemented so well as at HMS GANGES.

Chapter 2.

Hard Times.

We were escorted across the road from HMS GANGES to a secondary base called The Annexe where we would remain for our first six weeks while we were kitted out. Amongst other things we had to do was to mark our names on every item of our kit and I was rather glad I had a fairly short name. We also undertook various tests and learned how to drill before being transferred to the main base where we would become grade one boys and receive a small pay rise. The most frightening thing to emerge from my point of view was made clear to us the following morning. Every boy accepted to train at Ganges was required to climb the mast up to the final cross stanchion, some thirty feet or so from the top and as the mast was 150 feet tall this was a frightening thought to someone like me not keen on heights. 'Nobody has to climb right to the top' the Petty Officer assured us, 'The last bit had to be shinned up, there are no ladders. The button on the top is just big enough to stand on and there is a lightning conductor on top. You would have to pull yourself out away from the mast to get over the overhang, it is not dangerous if you take care and there is a large safety net if you should fall, but as I said that bit is optional.' It certainly wasn't an option to me and although some of my colleagues offered me various financial incentives there was no way I could be tempted.

It absolutely amazed me that anybody could shin up a pole with no ladder, 150 feet above ground and perch themselves right on the top. Even the thought of it frightened the life out of me. One of my closest friends from those early days was Peter Preston. A few months younger than me he thoroughly enjoyed climbing the mast and it wasn't long before he had made it to the top and sat on the button. 'It's a lovely view Dave' he said, but when I was climbing I usually had my eyes closed! A year before we arrived, Ganges was blessed with a new swimming pool. It was up to Olympic standard and somewhere I could always be found in my spare time. Being a competent swimmer I found it an ideal place to relax. Peter was not so lucky and I spent some time trying to teach him to swim. Non-swimmers had a hard time trying to learn often being thrown in at the deep end and told to learn or drown. If they struggled to the side the Instructors would stand on their fingers and force them back into the water. One of the most fantastic developments at HMS Ganges was the hospital wing, though I was fortunate not to see it at close quarters during my training We had an operating theatre up to the standard of most civilian hospitals with every type of medical equipment available and a Surgeon Captain fully trained to perform an array of operations. Wards and nursing staff completed the picture and the whole thing was situated on top of the cliff overlooking Harwich Harbour. It was wonderful to behold and we were all very proud of our Hospital Wing. Another ominous occurrence took place in 1939, when with another world war threatening we were all issued with gas masks and prepared for service at sea against the German Navy. During my fifteen months training at HMS GANGES, I was subjected to every type of stress imaginable and I must confess I was counting the days to the end of my course. I was determined to pass my exams first time as the thought of being re-coursed terrified me. I had finally conquered the mast climbing and although it made me feel quite faint I decided to get it out of the way as soon as possible so nothing could divert my attention from my course. The sport in Ganges was excellent. Each division could play each other at Football, Rugby, Cricket and many other sports while sailing up and down the River Stour was my particular favourite. Everything was competitive and I felt sorry for anyone who did not like Sport. Just when I began to think I would never leave Ganges my course was s completed and both Peter and myself passed our exams with honours, it was time for him and me to part company.

Chapter 3.

Preparation for War.

It was 1940 and we were at war once again with Germany. The Royal Navy urgently needed trained communication personnel and I was required to take a quick crash specialist training course at HMS Mercury before being drafted to my first ship. I finally said goodbye to Ganges with mixed feelings and looked back at the receding coastline with a host of memories. I once heard it described as 'Like a hospital,' 'A wonderful place to have as long as you never have to go there.' Later in 1944, I heard a boy fell from the top of the mast, hit a cross stanchion and was thrown outside the safety net underneath before hurtling across the road and through the roof of the station Post Office, needless to say, he was pronounced dead at the scene. The action was hotting up now with ships being sunk every day and as long as you knew a little about Radio Communications you were in, you could learn as you went along. I was drafted to serve in HMS Prince of Wales, a newly built battleship, so urgently needed that she sailed with a number of dockyard workers still on board completing the work. She was the pride of the fleet and a few eyebrows were raised when we were ordered to take on the Bismarck, said to be the unsinkable pride of the German fleet. We were to accompany HMS Hood in a supporting role and would surely not be needed in combat. She was confidently expected to sink the German ship single-handed. It was all over very quickly, Hood got a couple of shells close to Bismarck before the latter replied but then it only took one of the German battleship's massive shells to land in the Magazine, piercing the Hood's armoured deck. Without any reply she exploded and sank within minutes, one of our best and newest ships destroyed so easily we all felt sick. It was so sudden that out of her compliment of fourteen hundred men the total survivors were two midshipmen and one rating. We were ordered to run, there was no point in sacrificing yet another ship. Other plans would have to be worked out to deal with Bismarck, we must fight another day but how on earth you dealt with a ship like that was something that concerned us all. After this, we were engaged in escorting convoys and engaging other German ships and our success restored our faith in Prince of Wales. Some two months later we were off the coast of Malaya in company with HMS Repulse when we came under attack from a squadron of Japanese aircraft. This time, there was nowhere to hide and nowhere to run, we both took a terrible beating for over an hour before, despite sending a number of Aircraft to the bottom, both our brave ships, proud members of the British fleet could take no more and the order to 'Abandon Ship' was given.

I had issued a mayday telling all ships in the area where we were and I remember thinking 'Dive overboard and swim away from the ship.' It probably saved my life and being a strong swimmer I was able to survive several hours in the water, unfortunately, those few of us still alive were picked up by a Japanese patrol before our own ships could get to us. I was just about all in when we were rescued and frankly I couldn't care less who got to us first, however in the cold light of day I realised that I was now a prisoner of war and in the eyes of the British Navy I was listed as 'Missing, presumed dead' like so many other sailors. However, you thought about it, 'my war' was effectively now over.

Chapter 4.

Peace at Last.

I was one of a motley collection of P.O.W.'s sent to a Japanese camp at an outpost securely hidden in the Jungle but ideally situated for escape attempts. So much so that we were warned that any attempt to escape would be futile and met with death at the hands of a firing squad. Nevertheless, several attempts were made, virtually all failed and a number of my fellow prisoners disappeared after being returned to the camp. We can only assume that our captors carried out their deadly threats. Personally, I opted for a quiet life, taking no chances. We heard rumours that the war was ending but with no contact from home we couldn't be sure they were true, we didn't even know how the conflict was going and we could only survive as best we could and hope for the best. Early in 1945, we were liberated and returned to the United

Kingdom. I felt I had experienced every type of horror in war and in peace and yet, amazingly I was still only 22 years old! I returned home to Liverpool for a spell of compassionate leave with my mother. My father had finally retired from the Royal Navy at the end of the war and whether from injury or boredom he had suffered two minor heart attacks before having a massive one that took his life. I helped my mother handle everything before settling her in a retirement home for she needed constant care and was in very poor health. I was becoming restless myself feeling the war had robbed me of my anticipated career and as the navy was being scaled down I successfully applied for a communications job in the Merchant Navy and found myself at sea again escorting some of the merchant convoys still travelling around our coast. The area was constantly being patrolled by Minesweepers to detect and rid our shoreline of floating mines and underwater obstructions. Everybody was happy with the new found peace and we went about our business with a determination and purpose.

We had a number of close encounters and on one occasion our skipper distinguished himself by saving the ship when he gently edged a mine away from the ship when it was no more than twelve inches from blowing us out of the water. It was a scary few minutes while he edged the mine along the side of the ship till it floated astern of us. We were at a standstill gently rising and dipping on the swell while most of the ship's company held their breath and said their prayers. Captain Brian Robertson relieved everybody when he said 'O.K. men she's clear, slow ahead.' It brought the biggest cheer of the day! It was then my job to inform the nearest Minesweeper of the location and leave the unenviable job of dealing with it to them. My career in the Merchant Navy spanned over 30 years. My mother had died in 1950 and when I was decommissioned in 1977 at the age of 55 I decided I didn't want to return to Liverpool, opting instead for Suffolk where my story really began. I bought a modest house in the country and soon purchased a little car deciding I wanted to pay my old training base a visit. I was to be bitterly disappointed. The White Ensign had been lowered for the last time on 28th. October the previous year, HMS GANGES was no more, the site was unoccupied and derelict. The main areas remained, that dreadful mast, the beautiful swimming pool I enjoyed so much, the Quarterdeck, long and short covered way, sports fields, Annexe and the Hospital, though all the equipment had gone. What a terrible waste, it was like a sleeping giant lying silent, decaying in its own memories, it just seemed a sad end to what had been a 74-year long proud history for over 150,000 Navy recruits.

Chapter 5.

Return to Base.

In the forthcoming months, it emerged that the Ganges complex had been bought by a consortium of businessmen and was to be developed as a sports training village aimed specifically at visitors from the Continent. They would train under experts while living in the same quarters as we had occupied all those years before. The facilities were certainly excellent for Football, Swimming and Cricket to name just a few. Part of the complex near the old Gymnasium had been rented to a company called Delta Firearms and because of the very real threat from the I.R.A., it was necessary to turn part of their premises into a flat where a member of staff could sleep and make sure their firearms were guarded night and day. I noticed an advertisement in the local paper for Security Guards for the Ganges site. The Delta section was not to be included, they would handle their own security. I was looking for a part time job and with my knowledge of the Ganges, it seemed ideal. After two interviews I was delighted to be told I had got the job. Apparently the big worry to the owners was twofold. From Spring to Autumn the site would hopefully be occupied by visitors most of the time requiring careful monitoring and secondly in Winter the site would be empty for most of the time but would still need patrolling and guarding. The whole thing appealed to me just fine and although the pay was poor, fortunately I was not too desperate for money and the thought of the one weekend each year when old Ganges boys came back with the Ganges Association for a couple of days to meet old friends and march past on the Parade Square filled me with excitement. So it came about I completed the full circle and took over the position of night security officer on duty at 7 pm on four consecutive nights till 7 am then three nights off. The routine would then be reversed for the following week. There would also be some day shifts available if I wanted them. I would be expected to go out on patrol three times each night, at 9 pm, 1 am. and 5 am. The first night I took over I didn't know where to go first. It was like meeting a long lost friend again. There were plenty of lights in the establishment and as there was a contingent of Belgian and

Swedish teenagers on board I was frequently met by youngsters wandering around or going or coming back from the local public house down by the river. The buildings behind my office had been converted into mini-casinos that housed every type of machine imaginable. When a party of visitors arrived each youngster was encouraged to deposit an amount of spending money with me. The money would be checked and placed in an envelope with their name on and each time they wanted some money they could come and draw some from the envelope, the new balance would be entered on the outside of the envelope and returned to my safe. I carried a stock of chocolate, sweets and soft drinks which the youngsters could buy but any alcohol required had to be purchased from outside at the Bristol Arms Public House who usually did a roaring trade. There were plenty of activities available with several Snooker and Pool tables and about three Table Tennis tables available so there was normally plenty of company for me. Of course, I realised it would be a different story when the site was not occupied and I wondered if I would be quite so happy when that happened, I would have to see. At the moment, it was a full-time job and there was no time to get bored. I felt very important in

my new position and having a security
guards uniform and a truncheon helped.

Chapter 6.

The Ganges Association.

After all the excitement of the young sportsmen subsided and we moved into November the Ganges site became very lonely. Bobby Rees, a young lad who worked for Delta often took the night duty and he made a practice of coming up to my office around 10 pm and joining me for a cup of coffee and a chat. This actually extended to several cups of coffee and a bit of television until around midnight when he would come out with me on patrol. He seemed to think that I needed his protection and always made a point of showing me his pistol. He never came without it and it was always loaded, 'Nothing frightens me' he would say but I often wondered what he would do if anyone confronted us, I honestly believe he would shoot first and ask questions afterwards. I must admit despite this I was glad of his company and we became good friends. Remembrance Sunday, the 11th November was to be the next Ganges Association and I was desperately hoping to meet my old friend Peter again. Every 'old boy' was invited to return to Ganges and accommodation was available if required so they could make a weekend of it. They would start arriving on Friday, many of them in their old sailor boys outfits with the famous pill-box hat. One of them took up his position outside the main gate in full uniform with his service rifle at the stand easy position coming to attention each time one of his old colleagues arrived. On Saturday morning, we were due to parade on the Parade Ground for the celebration of 'Sunrise' after which we were free to look round. Breakfast would be available but otherwise, the day was free. That evening we were invited to a social evening in the Wardroom with refreshments and plenty of drink while various entertainments were arranged. I couldn't help smiling when two of the old boys met. It seemed as though everybody was carrying a hip flask and they would swap their flasks inviting each other to 'take a swig.' The main events were reserved for the Sunday. We were to form up on the Parade Ground before the marchpast and then to be taken by transport to Shotley Village Church for the Remembrance Day service; after which we would perform an act of remembrance both in the old Ganges section of the graveyard and in the more modern Naval Cemetery. Returning to Ganges we would be invited to lunch in the Wardroom and everybody would be welcome to look round all their old haunts before dispersing during the afternoon. It was during the Friday afternoon that my heart missed a beat. There he was, he had hardly changed over the years, I recognised him at once, my old friend Peter Preston. We had so much to talk about we almost missed the tea laid on for us in the Wardroom.

The following day we were walking round together when he came out with a strange request. 'David' he said, 'Could we have a look at the swimming pool?' 'It's derelict and closed up' I replied, 'Many of the glass panels in the roof fell down in a storm and it isn't safe to go in, anyway there's no water in it now.' 'I just want to see it' he replied, 'Please David' I called at my office and drew the keys and we both moved quietly into the swimming pool. Only the noise of the birds broke the eerie silence. 'Could you please leave me on my own for a few minutes' he pleaded and I decided to grant his wish. Rejoining him I found him as white as a sheet and quickly led him out into the winter sunshine. Peter explained that his younger brother Bobby had drowned there in 1944. He couldn't swim and Peter wondered how it happened. 'I heard his voice Dave' my friend insisted 'Begging to be helped out of the water.' 'It was your imagination' I replied. 'He called me Pip' Peter shouted, 'It was his nickname for me, nobody else ever called me that.' I was badly shaken.

Chapter 7

Things Start Going Wrong.

It was two weeks after 'Ganges weekend' that I got my first surprise. I am certainly not of a nervous disposition, neither do I believe in the supernatural, I feel that after my lifetimes experiences I have gradually got to believe that everything has a place and a sensible explanation. It was as I left my office for my second patrol just after midnight. It was a comparatively simple thing of no great significance nevertheless a bit strange. My friend from Delta was not with me, being a Friday night he had gone home for the weekend. His replacement, a man in his fifties was not the type to come to my office preferring instead to watch television in Delta before turning in around 11 pm. It was a very windy night as I recall and there was an abundance of noises as roof slates on the old buildings sighed and heaved as they moved around. I was walking across the Quarterdeck when suddenly there was a loud bang. Somewhere down the Long Covered Way as a door had blown open and was banging in the stiff wind. At first, I felt inclined to ignore it but its continued noise began to irritate me and I decided to find and secure it. Shining my torch one by one on the multitude of billet doors down the Long Covered Way I gradually found my way down towards the river below. Bang, the offensive door continued to blow to and fro in the wind until I reached the bottom without finding it.

I stopped and listened intently to get another position for it but found to my surprise the banging was not coming from around me but from the direction of the Quarterdeck, where I had just come from. Puzzled, I retraced my steps more determined than ever to find the culprit. Just before I reached the top of the Long Covered Way I stopped again to check on its location. Bang, it was still maintaining its momentum only now, surely not, it was clearly coming from the direction of The Petty Officers Mess on the other side of the Parade Ground. I stopped to think. It was ridiculous but there was no doubt about it, that's where it was. Determined not to be beaten I crossed the Parade Ground and made for the Petty Officers Mess, coming to a halt before

entering it and cocking my head as I sorted
out the necessary keys. The wind had
dropped slightly but I could still discern the
banging door but, impossible as it seemed
the noise was now coming from the
direction of the Wardroom. I felt I was
going mad but decided not to resume the
search but to monitor the noise as I made my
patrol around the site. The banging
continued but I never seemed to track it
down, wherever I was the door seemed to be
in another part of the site. I eventually got
fed up with the whole thing, it seemed to be
mocking me and I returned to my office for
a cup of coffee. I could still hear it but
closed and locked my door to shut it out. I
would make the following observation. I am
certain I heard just one door banging and I
could only put the episode down to the
empty buildings, perhaps the echoes that can
be heard around HMS GANGES and to a
lesser degree, my own tiredness. I sat back
in my chair and closed my eyes. This place
took a lot of getting used to just as it did all
those years before. It had a mind of its own
and refused to conform to normality, so
what had changed? My alarm went off and
woke me with a start. It was 5 am and time
for my last patrol of the night. I stretched
and shook the sleep from my eyes.
Collecting my bunch of keys I pulled my

coat around my ears and opened my office door. The wind was still quite strong and paper and rubbish was blowing around the site. As I stepped out into the cold morning air I immediately heard it. Bang, that door was still performing. I had to smile, it was coming from the direction of the Long Covered Way. I must confess I turned my head towards the noise and quietly mouthed a few words, I can't repeat them!

Chapter 8.

A Spell of Day Shifts.

I was relieved at 7 am and decided not to mention my experience to my relief it seemed too trivial and silly. I was off duty on the Saturday and Sunday and due to resume day shifts on the Monday morning through Tuesday and Wednesday before having Thursday off and re-starting night shifts on Thursday evening. There was nobody in but evidence had been found to suggest that somebody had been sleeping rough in the Hospital Block. 'I'll keep an eye on things and let you know if we find anything else before you take over on Thursday night Dave' John said, 'Have a nice break.' I enjoyed a quiet weekend at home which was just as well as the weather had broken up becoming wet, windy and very cold. Monday morning I returned for duty to be told no further evidence had been found to suggest a trespasser was on board and I decided it was perhaps time I went and took a closer look at the Hospital Block in daylight having only seen it from the outside once since taking up my security duties. It really was a formidable complex and though derelict I could imagine what it had been like in its heyday. I decided to look round the wards and what had been the operating theatre. I went to push open the heavy metal doors but found to my surprise that they didn't move. There didn't appear to be any bolt across between them and I was pretty sure they were not locked. I put a bit more weight behind my effort and pushed the door again. It was then that I heard it. Just audible above the fairly brisk wind coming in across the harbour I heard it clearly. 'What do you want?' So that was it, someone was inside, probably the someone said to be sleeping rough inside the Hospital Block. Before I could answer the same voice spoke again. 'Do you come in peace?' it asked, 'Yes' I answered, 'I mean you no harm.' To my astonishment, there was no sound of locks or bolts being withdrawn but the doors opened at once. A quick examination told me there was no key in the doors and I moved cautiously inside. There was no obvious evidence that anybody had been there and I moved from one building to another taking in the vastness of the Hospital Block. It was enormous and I could imagine what it had been like when it was operational all those years before. There was no sign of anybody in the buildings and when I left I opened the outside doors easily. I felt totally rattled. I didn't believe in the supernatural but what on earth had I just heard? The whole thing happened just as I have described it and, by the way, I had not had a drink at the time though I certainly needed a stiff one shortly afterwards. A fortnight later an S.A.S. Officer stayed on site for a week as he frequently did and he walked round with me on a number of occasions.

On one such trip, I deliberately led him down to the Hospital Wing and up to the main doors. I went to push them open but he put a hand on my arm. The doors were to all intents and purposes locked. He spoke without hesitation 'We come in peace' he announced quite clearly. The doors quietly opened and we went in. I looked at him in astonishment. 'It's alright' he assured me 'I found out some time ago the spirits don't take kindly to being disturbed. If ever you want to get in just say what I said and they'll let you in.' I must confess I didn't accept his explanation but on numerous occasions, it has been proved correct. 'Many boys died here years ago from diphtheria and scarlet fever, their spirits live on inside.' he said 'I don't think anyone would want to sleep rough in here' I replied, 'I'd rather sleep on the grass outside.'

Chapter 9.

More Shocks.

After this, I rarely went near the Hospital Block. I couldn't accept his explanation yet I couldn't find one of my own neither credible nor otherwise. Thursday evening, I was still trying to come to terms with what had happened when I received another surprise. On my first patrol around 9 pm, I came across a light on, deep in the middle of the main Galley. This building was no longer in use except for a couple of rooms used for storage purposes in the middle of the C.M.G. I had to return to my office and collect the massive bunch of keys that covered all the rooms inside the C.M.G. Returning again I had to use several keys to work my way into the middle of the building until I found the offending room. Opening it I was surprised to find the switch was an old fashioned round one that was quite difficult to put on and off so it could not have come on accidentally. I extinguished it and made my way back through the building locking all the doors individually. The whole operation took several minutes but, at least, the light was out. Imagine my amazement when three hours later, on my second patrol I found that the same light was on again! This time, I left it on and informed my relief when handing over at 7 am. 'That's always happening' he answered. 'Is it on a time switch?' I asked, 'Good heavens No' he replied, 'Nobody knows why it comes on, just leave it' There were other lights that came on and went out when it suited them and I soon got to know which ones they were. On another occasion, I found all the lights from the top to the bottom of the Long Covered Way burning brightly on my second patrol and decided I would have to put them all out individually as there was no master switch. Starting at the bottom I had only come a quarter the way up and extinguished three or four of the lights when suddenly all the remaining lights went out at once.

Again I can offer no explanation or reason. The greatest shock was still to come the following week when on my first patrol I met a young man I didn't know. 'Who are you?' I demanded. 'My name is John' he replied, 'I've replaced Bobby Rees at Delta, he left last week.' 'Why?' I enquired, 'He seemed to be quite happy in his job.' 'I think he was' John answered, 'Until one night he got up in the middle of the night to go to the toilet. Apparently when he returned along the corridor to go back to his room he thought he saw a man standing at the end of the corridor with his back to him. He challenged him asking what he was doing there and the man turned round. He was dressed in old time sailors clothes from the first world war had a long beard and a telescope under his arm. Bobby shouted 'Stand where you are' but the man smiled and walked straight through the outside door despite the fact that it was locked. Bobby pumped the contents of his pistol into the door to no avail, the man had gone. On checking he found the door locked and properly secured, Bobby was so scared he up and left right away. I don't think he ever recovered.' 'Aren't you scared? ' I asked him. 'Good heavens No' he replied, 'I don't believe in ghosts, he was obviously half asleep and imagined the whole thing. Even if ghosts did exist what good would a pistol be?' He struck me as a more sensible lad than Bobby though I wondered how long it would be before he had to revise his views.

Certainly after my recent experiences, I couldn't believe he wasn't in for a surprise somewhere along the way in the not too distant future.

Chapter 10.

Leave them in Peace.

Whether or not my recent experiences had any effect on me I don't know but after everything that had happened, I found I was not so keen to go on patrol as I was supposed to especially at night. I couldn't believe I was allowing these things to get to me. Despite my lifetime view that ghosts did not exist I was beginning to believe that there was something beyond our comprehension happening here in HMS GANGES. I began to imagine I could hear screams coming from the swimming pool and every time I walked past the Post Office building adjacent to Nelson Hall and the Parade Square I swore I could see the different colours of the slates on the roof. The main area of the roof was old and the grey slates were green with moss and years of wear while the area around the middle of the roof near the old chimney was much newer with slates of a darker shade of grey. Instinctively I found myself looking up at the formidable Ganges mast and imagined I could see a young sailor boy falling from the top

Nine times out of ten the boy would land in the safety net but at the tenth, the lad would hit the wooden Cross member, be thrown outwards beyond the net, across the road and through the roof of the Post Office. Obviously the injuries sustained were almost always fatal. . I even found myself waking up at night in a cold sweat. The dream was always the same and ended with a horrible scream. Things couldn't go on the way they were. I began to hate night shifts and found myself making excuses to get off them in favour of daytime shifts. The screams never seemed to worry me during the day but still came back to haunt me at home as I desperately tried to get some sleep. . My boss had noticed a change in me and offered to share a couple of night shifts with me to see what was wrong. I gratefully accepted his offer and gradually explained what was going on in my mind. He was most understandable and offered to share a week of night shifts with me to see if I could get over my fears. While he was with me nothing untoward happened, we even visited the Hospital Block and entered it without any problem. I began to think I was imagining everything and by the end of the week I declared I felt much better about everything. I apologised to him and said I would like to carry on with my job and go back to nights. 'Good for you' he replied and the next night I took up my shift at 7 o'clock as usual. I went out on my first patrol at 9 pm and found no lights on and nothing unusual. I was feeling much better in myself and felt convinced that I had got over my fears. After several cups of coffee and a couple of hours television, I prepared for the midnight patrol full of confidence. It was as I was leaving the Quarterdeck and heading for the Parade Ground that it happened. I couldn't believe it but there was a figure walking under the safety net beneath the mast. I moved smartly to intercept him only to lose sight of him once again. I was under the mast when suddenly I saw him again crossing the Quarterdeck, though how on earth he got past me I couldn't imagine. I doubled back and chased him past the Wardroom and he ran into the tennis courts beyond. There was no escape now as they were surrounded by a 12-foot wire fence. I flexed my truncheon; I had him now and wanted to see what he had to say. 'Stand still,' I shouted. To my amazement, he turned and walked straight through the wire as though it wasn't there heading off towards faith, hope and charity and the steps leading down to the river. I was shaking like a leaf, it couldn't happen and yet it had. I didn't know what kind of phenomenon occupied the Ganges but whatever it was it demanded to be left alone, I had no intention of denying it that right. I handed in my notice next morning and with the exception of one weekend, each year, I would never enter HMS GANGES again.

The Legend of the Headless Horseman.

Myth or fact this unusual legend really exists in many rural areas.

For many a year Headless Horsemen and Ghostly Horses have terrified the locals and to this day gathered around the fire of a country inn the stories are still told.....

The Headless Horseman

Chapter 1.

The Beginning

I was born in the midlands and after a normal childhood I became a keen scholar at school but as I progressed to manhood I began to take an interest in the paranormal. I constantly searched for and visited places renowned for ghostly happenings regretfully with virtually no success. The occasional unexplained noise was almost all I could find to satisfy my longing for the supernatural and I was completely unable to come across any ghostly apparitions. Despite this, I refused to give up and still believed in ghosts certain that they were out there and one day I would find the answer to what I was searching for. Then one day I read an article in my local paper about a headless horseman who was supposed to appear regularly at Halloween on October 31st. every year and it caught my imagination. This event apparently occurred in East Anglia in a little village called Shotley, ten miles or so from Ipswich. So I packed a case and assembled my equipment, loaded everything into the old Ford and set off for the East coast where this apparition was supposed to appear. Giving myself a couple of weeks to prepare I arrived at my destination on October 15th and had a look around the area. The headless horseman was said to travel in a carriage led by two black horses from the old rectory at Shotley to a house called Erwarton Hall, a distance of just under a mile along a track known locally as Erwarton Walk. I easily found the Old Rectory and the track to the big house which a local farmer told me was Erwarton Hall. In answer to my question of where I could find somewhere to stay he pointed me beyond the Hall to a little country public house called the Queens Head in Erwarton village no more than a mile further on, it seemed ideal. Although they were not recognised for offering accommodation the landlord said he would be able to help me and I duly booked in. It was a lovely little place with a big log fire and a liberal supply of local ale and first class food and whatever happened I began to believe this was one assignment I was going to enjoy. Several local farm labourers came in regularly for their evening pint and I enjoyed chatting with them One or two insisted they had seen the carriage with the headless horseman, but their descriptions varied so much, that I gradually realised none of them had actually seen it but were revelling in the attention I was giving them, however, everybody seemed convinced the stories were genuine. Apparently the carriage came out of Shotley rectory and travelled along Erwarton Walk to Erwarton Hall at exactly midnight on October 31st. each year.

Some of the locals thought the event was something to do with Anne Boleyn's heart which was buried in the village church just down the road from the Hall. Local opinion also was sure there was an underground tunnel from the Hall to the rectory where somebody had to flee for their life although again opinion as to who it was and when it took place differed considerably. All this information only served to increase my interest and I decided it was necessary to take a close look at both places before Halloween and consider how best to approach this matter. Accordingly I walked from the pub to Erwarton Hall, a distance of about a mile and a half shortly after dark. The locals were quite sure the place was uninhabited and belonged to some rich baron in London who was hardly ever there. I climbed over an old style farm gate and looked up at the massive house, it was some three or four storeys high and in the moonlight, it looked very large and foreboding. Standing in about four acres of land that was mostly down to grass with a good collection of outbuildings there were two entrances to the grounds which were both securely locked the house itself was in fairly good condition. The doors and windows all appeared to be secure and there was no indication that anybody was there. I walked around the house to the back and suddenly stood perfectly still. The late harvest moon was quite bright and I had no need for the trusty torch I carried but suddenly I could have sworn I saw a light in one of the upper windows. It could have been a trick of the moonlight and I was unable to see it anymore so after a few minutes I felt satisfied that it was probably my imagination so I worked my way round to the front of the house once again before deciding to leave the place and continue along Erwarton Walk in the opposite direction to that which the carriage was said to take making my way towards Shotley rectory. Local opinion assured me that this place was occupied by the parish priest and I had to be very careful about going into the grounds. I also understood that he had two rather dangerous dogs that I had no wish to meet. I felt it was necessary to get to know the layout of the place and once that was done I would leave as discreetly as possible. It was time to exercise the utmost care and make as little noise as possible. Fortunately, the moon was bright enough for me to find my way around without using my torch.

Chapter 2.

The Old Rectory.

The rectory was a different proposition to the Hall occupying a corner site between Erwarton Walk and the main Ipswich to Shotley road. The amount of ground it covered was very similar to the Hall but this was surrounded by a thick hedge some six foot high with many old and very tall trees. There were two entrances, the main one on the Shotley road with another round the back coming out on to Erwarton Walk, this would obviously be the way the carriage would come out. Also included in the grounds were a large pond well overgrown and lawns and a tennis court. Behind the main area was a well kept vegetable garden leading to a number of out buildings. There were lights on in the house in several rooms confirming the occupants were at home and I was careful how I made my way to look at the outbuildings moving quietly and very slowly. These comprised three very large sheds all fairly modern looking and securely locked adjoined by what looked like a stable block which much to my surprise was unlocked. I moved quietly into the building and shone my torch carefully around the walls. All sorts of riding gear hung there while several pairs of riding boots were laid out beneath them. Moving into the main part of the stable block I couldn't help feeling excited as I came across a double horse carriage appearing to be fairly new with the black paint on it glistening in the torchlight. I guessed the horses were housed in the other buildings and certainly everything in this place was arranged in a very neat and tidy manner. A quick look around the corners failed to produce any further equipment that might help to realise this was the carriage concerned but I had to admit it was exactly what I had expected it to look like. My fears were suddenly alerted by a dog barking loudly and although there was no proof that it was one of the owners I decided it was not worth taking the risk, it was time to go and I quietly left by the same route I had come in by and returned to the Queens Head. My visit had been quite promising and I felt I had done enough for one night anyway. I made good time with the thought of a welcome pint driving me on and I was soon back to the warm atmosphere of the bar where a number of locals were already enjoying their evening. Apparently there was a dart match arranged and the place was noisier than usual but my arrival caused a stir among the locals who wanted to know what I had found and soon the conversation turned once again to the headless horseman. Everybody was quite amazed when they found out I had been in and out of the grounds of both the old buildings and they wanted to know what I had found.

'I think I've found the horse carriage' I announced 'Though as it's still only the 23rd of October and it will be over another week before anything is likely to happen'. One of the locals then captured my attention by saying he had seen a ghost ship sail up the River Orwell late at night just before Christmas last year. There was very little traffic on the river and the appearance of the ship caused quite a lot of interest particularly as it only appeared at night and seemed to sail in complete silence up the river towards Ipswich keeping fairly close to the Shotley side while not showing the usual riding lights. Rumor had it that she dropped anchor somewhere off Woolverstone and stayed for about an hour before retracing her steps back out to sea. Felixstowe Dock was hardly in being in those days and nobody seemed to take any notice of her activities. I made a mental note to follow this one up after Halloween feeling I had done enough for one night, it was time to follow the darts match and enjoy the excitement. The old country boys certainly liked their darts and were far too good for their opponents. I got caught up in the atmosphere and thoroughly enjoyed the evening. The next three nights were taken up with further visits to both the old houses while I managed a daytime visit to the village church to give me an insight into the fact that Anne Boleyn's heart was buried in the building. There was certainly no shortage of history in this part of the world and as I ticked off the day's towards the end of October I felt a great deal of excitement and apprehension as to what would actually happen, I was certainly due some more success than I had received up to now but would I really see the black double horse-drawn carriage driven by a headless horseman and if so what did it all mean? Was there any sense in any of it, would anyone believe it if he really saw it? Fortunately, I had brought a piece of equipment that would surely prove beyond doubt exactly what happened on that night and it was comforting to know that whatever happened would be caught on film for everyone to see. I found the excitement building up and even the extra incentive of two or three pints of the excellent local brew every night failed to help me sleep as we gradually got nearer to the end of October and Halloween.

Chapter 3.

Halloween.

Tuesday, October 31st. dawned wet and windy with a forecast that the weather would not improve much at all that day. I rose early and checked my equipment which consisted of a powerful torch and the latest camera that I could set to record whatever happened, also, there was a pair of thick boots and wet weather gear to protect me from the elements.

I left the Queens Head a little after nine o'clock in the evening and had a quick look round the old Hall where everything was more or less the same as on the previous occasion. On rounding the building to the front of the property I stopped in horror. Although the moonlight left a lot to be desired nevertheless there was no doubt whatsoever that the large gates at the entrance which had been securely shut and locked on my last visit were now wide open. I saw no further light in the old building and nothing else seemed to have been touched except for those gates. Leaving the property I made my way along Erwarton Walk to the Shotley rectory where again things were very much the same as on my last visit until I found my way round to the outbuildings and here once again a shock awaited me, although the doors to the sheds were once more securely locked the stable building was unlocked and the doors were wide open. Just inside the double doors, the carriage was silently waiting and it appeared to be prepared for a journey with several items of riding gear that had been hanging on the wall now taken down and placed beside the carriage. There was still no sign of the horses or the riders but everything else suggested the carriage was going for a trip. I took a quick look at my watch and noticed it was only just after quarter past ten so there was still almost two hours to go before midnight. I realised I was breathing much faster as I began to feel I really was going to see the headless horseman. For the first time since my arrival in East Anglia I felt confident that there was some truth in the rumour and things would not be happening as they were unless he was going to appear and if he did I had got the right equipment to make sure I could prove to everybody that the myth was really fact. I quickly retraced my steps and left the grounds of the old rectory through the rear entrance to return to my chosen position on Erwarton Walk. By the time I had arrived and set up the camera making sure it was placed where it would get the best possible pictures it was twenty past eleven, not long to go now. The wind seemed even stronger and the moonlight a little fader while there was also drizzly rain to contend with, I hoped the moon did not go behind a cloud at the vital time though there was nothing I could do to prevent it happening, even as things stood visibility was poorer than I would have liked. I turned the camera up to full power and switched it on. It was approaching quarter to twelve and I was finally all ready, if the headless horseman put in an appearance then I would see him and get a picture to prove he really does exist. Double checking everything was working I took up my position in the middle of Erwarton Walk. All was quiet except for the howling wind though even that appeared to have moderated a little.

My watch showed almost five minutes to

twelve and I was sure it was right as I had checked it earlier and set it to give off a buzzer alarm at exactly midnight. I was looking at my watch constantly now as the luminous minute hand crept nearer to the top of the hour, it seemed ages since I had left the Queens Head and I wondered if some of the old boys were thinking of me now. I was standing in the middle of the lane and waited as the hand approached midnight. Suddenly it was there and all hell let loose deafening the silence of the night. Instantaneously the alarm went off and I saw a horse drawn carriage coming straight towards me in the moonlight. The two horses were neighing and the driver cracking his whip. I had to physically throw myself to one side to avoid being run down and as it was the wheels of the carriage only missed me by inches as the crazed beasts flew like lightning through the night. I managed to get a quick look at the driver though he was well wrapped up against the weather, he had what looked like a thick full-length coat on with a high drawn hood on top of it but was he headless? I couldn't be sure because I wasn't able to pick out any facial features; the whole thing was over in seconds as he disappeared in the direction of Erwarton Hall. My heart was beating at an incredible rate as I realised how close I came to being run down and almost certainly killed by the carriage, thank goodness for the camera, at least, that would show exactly what happened. There was nothing else to be done here and I packed up my things and set off for the warm atmosphere of the Queens Head. I had told them I would be late and they promised me they would wait up for me with a large glass of whisky. A quick glance at the Hall told me the front gates were now shut as I turned towards the rain and set off for the Queens Head.

Chapter 4.

The Camera doesn't lie,- does it?

On arriving at the pub I gladly drank the glass of whisky and felt my body warmth gradually returning. The landlord and landlady joined me in my room and the three of us waited excitedly as I set up the camera to play back what had happened on the big screen I had prepared before leaving. We could hardly contain ourselves feeling we were about to solve the mystery at long last. We were all staring intently at the screen as the camera started to whir. There I was setting it up before moving into the middle of the lane after which there was a short break before the buzzing of the alarm as midnight arrived, suddenly I flung myself to the side to avoid being run down and now for the carriage, but where was the carriage?

It was simply not there, absolutely nothing

was there, the film was completely blank, no carriage, no horses, no horseman, headless or otherwise, I couldn't believe it. If I'd have stayed where I was in the middle of the lane I am quite sure it would have hit me, or would it? I began to wonder. I firmly believe that I had seen the headless horseman and the carriage drawn by two black horses and nobody will ever convince me that I am wrong but alas I have no proof. The ghostly apparition could not be filmed so did it really exist? It would be another twelve months before the event was due to happen again and perhaps the result would be the same, who knows. I found sleep hard to come by and tossed around for a few hours before daylight thankfully came to my rescue and I got up. The landlord was very philosophical, suggesting it was perhaps wise not to interfere with the powers of the abnormal but I couldn't bring myself to agree with him and after a good breakfast I set off once again for the old Hall where nothing appeared to have changed. I intended to go up to the rectory again but not in daylight, it was too dangerous. There was no sign of the carriage or horses and the front gates were once again firmly locked shut. Suddenly my heart missed a beat, even though the gates were shut, just inside them was something that had not been there before. It came immediately to my attention, a horse had certainly been through the gates since last night, of that there could be absolutely no doubt and, however eerie the whole thing seemed, at least, one of the horses was real, for there before me was the most beautiful piece of horse manure you could imagine. It really was proof indeed that something had happened last night. However mysterious, at least one of the horses was perfectly alive. I returned to the Queen's Head for lunch and spent a lazy afternoon before leaving for the old rectory making sure it would be dark before I arrived. Once more, for the last time, I told myself I slipped through the rear entrance into the grounds and found my way round to the outbuildings which, as I expected were once again securely locked with the exception of the stable block which as usual was unlocked though the doors were this time closed. I entered the building and found my way through to the area where the carriage had stood but it was no longer there. Also, the riding gear that hung round the walls was missing suggesting the carriage was still away. I smiled to myself, however mysterious the whole thing was I would never know the answer. I considered calling on the residents but decided against it, after all what could I say? After a last look around I closed the doors and made my way out through the rear exit for what would I was sure to be the last occasion. It was time to go back to the Queens Head for my final night and as I expected, the locals all wanted to know what happened the previous night. What I told them left them disappointed but I assured them the legend of the headless horseman was in my opinion all fact and somebody else would one day succeed in proving it.

Woolverstone Cathouse.

Many years ago smuggling did take place at this quiet country location and a white cat was used to tell the smugglers when the coast was clear. Many barrels of spirits and beer were brought ashore in this way. To this day, the cat still appears in the window of the cottage

Woolverstone Cat House.

Chapter 1.

The Cat's in charge.

I'm Brian Bates, and my early days were happy and carefree living as I did, in the heart of East Anglia. My mother and father lived in a small cottage on the farm where he worked near the River Orwell at a place called Woolverstone in Suffolk. The cottage came with his job at Mannings Farm and a more beautiful setting I could not imagine. From my very earliest days I loved the countryside and the area leading down to the river where I spent almost all of my time. I had absolutely no fear of messing about on the .water despite one or two close calls when I came close to drowning after falling out of an old boat belonging to my father

My parents were horrified and begged me to be more careful but I took very little noice of their concerns. My early school days were spent at the tiny Woolverstone Primary School which prepared me for my secondary education at Holbrook Secondary Modern school where I became interested in every type of sport.

I trained hard and gradually obtained a well-built physique that stood me in good stead to handle myself. I stood head and shoulders above my school mates and quickly found a permanent position in the school rugby and football teams. Unfortunately, I was never one of the brightest students and found Maths and English two subjects well beyond me.

My mother died when I was just approaching school leaving age and my father took early retirement. Never really getting over mother's death he left me to take over his work as farm manager, ensuring we could continue to live in the cottage. The Land owning farmer was no doubt well satisfied to have a younger, fitter, labourer who could do the work of two men if required to do so. I had never shown much interest in the fairer sex which had seemed to pique my parents and I had no interest in pubs and clubs while theatres never appealed either. I became a bit of a loner happy to spend my time roaming the countryside with Tyke, my dog, climbing trees and shooting the pheasants and rabbits which hung about around our cottage looking for food. My father's health deteriorated without his wife to look after him as he gradually took less and less care of himself not eating enough and drinking far too much. He was obviously heading downhill and it was no surprise when he passed away just over twelve months after my mother's death and I took over as the legal tenant of the cottage. I was now living alone but it never bothered me and I was quite happy sharing the place with Tyke. Weeks and months passed quickly and it was around early September when I was to have a visitor. This was a very unusual event, especially in the evening. It turned out to be a middle-aged man who introduced himself as John Randall and he had come to offer me a part time job, about two hours a night as and when required to supplement my existing day job. It would be well paid and there would be no travelling involved. Apparently he represented a small consortium that took delivery of barrels of oil that came in by boat at Woolverstone periodically and required delivering locally. It was the cheapest way to get the goods delivered. They came from abroad on specific dates and I would be notified when a consignment was due. The barrels were to be brought ashore by his team of men and delivered locally by horse and carriage. 'It's heavy work' he said 'but with your strength, I'm sure you could do it easily.' Apparently one of his team had put his back out when he slipped over in the water while carrying a barrel and he'd been unable to work since. 'We heard of you and we needed someone with plenty of strength, are you interested?' I certainly was and decided to give it a go. The next delivery was coming in on the following Tuesday at 10pm and I agreed to meet them there. 'All you'll need is a good pair of waterproof thigh boots and a thick coat to wrap up against the weather; I'll see you there then.' I found I was looking forward to the experience and could hardly wait for the weekend to pass. I prepared myself with a waterproof top and trousers and with my trusty waterproof thigh boots I felt I was well protected whatever the weather. Tuesday dawned wet and windy with little change expected all day and we had a comparatively quiet day at work and I decided to leave my tea until later than usual and stepping into my boots I put out the light and set off for the waterfront at Woolverstone in good time to be joined by three other strong looking young men and Mr. Randall all well dressed up against the weather. Nothing happened for a while until one of the lads spoke out.

'Here she comes' he said, 'Bang on time as usual.' Gradually a long dark shape glided into view, our boat had arrived.

Chapter 2.

Unloading gets Underway.

It was difficult to pick out the boat as the moon had passed behind a cloud and there were no riding lights showing on her anywhere. Mr. Randall barked out an order. 'Wait for it lads, the cat's not out yet.' I wondered what on earth he meant but suddenly a light went on in one of the windows in a cottage overlooking the river. The window had a large white cat painted on it and that was the signal for us to start work walking into the water and making our way towards the boat.

'Keep to the hard' Mr. Randall instructed while the boat quickly tied up to a pole obviously placed there for that purpose. The barrel that was passed to me was heavy but certainly not beyond my capabilities and I carried it easily ashore before setting it down beside an old cart with a horse obviously anxious to get going. I was fascinated by the way the team worked together and I returned for a second barrel. Three or four more trips and the unloading was complete. Mr. Randall was very pleased and passed an envelope to a man who was obviously the skipper of the boat who shook hands with him before casting off and waving goodbye to us. Slowly the boat drifted off towards Felixstowe and the open sea its voyage over. The light in the window where the white cat had been was suddenly extinguished and quietness returned again to the waterfront. The whole operation was over very quickly and we were all offered a glass of rum to keep out the cold and although not a drinking man I felt I needed that and gratefully drank it down. I helped to load some of the barrels into the cart before being told my night's work was over and being passed ten pounds for my efforts. I was delighted and together with an older man moved away from the waterfront to make my way home.

'What was that all about?' I asked him.

'That was oil' he replied, 'Mostly for garages to enable them to build a future range of motor vehicles.'

'But I noticed different letters on the barrels I carried' I persisted, 'One had a 'B' on it another an 'R' and a third had a 'W' what did that all mean?'

'Different grades' he replied, 'Light oil suitable for a specific purpose, medium grade, and a thicker type, I've no idea what the letters stand for. Mr. Randall said it was nothing to do with us, we do a job and get paid for it and we need not concern ourselves with anything else.'

'And what about the Cat?' I asked.

'It's some kind of signal' he said 'we don't unload until the cat appears in the window.' It all sounded very mysterious but we had arrived at my cottage by now and I now bade him good night. I had completed my first consignment of oil although I couldn't't help feeling a little doubtful about his explanation, however, the money was handy. I wondered who lived in the cottage where the cat was in the window, was it someone who knew the whereabouts of the local policeman or perhaps it was the local custodian of the law himself who was in on the operation for it seemed to me the whole thing suggested it was in some way illegal. With these thoughts I prepared for a rather later than usual night's sleep noting my clock suggested it was just after one o'clock, I would be tired in the morning. At least, Tyke was glad to see me, he must have been wondering if he had needed to spend the night on his own, something he obviously wasn't very keen on and he soon curled up in the middle of my bed before I shoved him roughly to one side.

After my experience, I heard nothing more from Mr. Randall for a couple of weeks and began to wonder if I had perhaps made a mess of my opportunity although I felt sure I had done everything he asked without making any mistakes. Had I spoken out of turn to the man I walked home with? Perhaps he felt I was beginning to pry into their operation and perhaps he would not use me again. I needn't have worried, however, just when I thought my short employment had come to an abrupt end Mr. Randall called to see me again. 'There's a delivery coming in tomorrow night' he began 'It's been arranged at very short notice, can you make it?' 'Of course I can,' I answered, 'what time?'

'Same as before' he replied 'About 10pm weather permitting, apparently the forecast isn't very good, anyway I'll see you there.' With that, he left to leave me alone with my thoughts. What was in those barrels? Somehow his explanation didn't make sense, there were hardly any motor vehicles about at the moment and they wouldn't need all that oil. Where were the barrels delivered? There were no shops anywhere on the peninsula and even if there were, they would not be open at that time of night, it really was a mystery. Was the operation legal? And if not could I be in trouble for taking part? I had never faced any charges for doing anything wrong before, what would my father have said I lost track of the radio programme I had been listening to. Perhaps it was time to have an early night with a hard day to come tomorrow followed by a late night. Tyke agreed so I put out the light and went to bed.

Chapter 3.

Another Consignment arrives.

The following day once again dawned wet and windy and made me think winter had finally arrived. The day's work on the farm was a bit heavier than usual with muck spreading on the agenda and us labourers having to spread the little heaps already left in rows over the field by hand using forks. By five o'clock I'd just about had enough and set off wearily for home smelling a bit like a sewer. A bath was obviously called for and I collected the old tin bath out of the shed. I was rather sorry I had taken on the extra job tonight but had no intention of letting Mr. Randall down and stoking up the fire I slid gracefully into the soothing water. It was soon time for tea and soup followed by bread and cheese was the order of the day after which I settled down in the old armchair and taking Tyke on my lap I dozed off.

The rest did me some good but I woke up with a start realising it was almost half past nine and pushing the old dog roughly to the floor I quickly gathered my wet weather gear and rushed out of the house arriving at the Quay at ten minutes to ten to meet a harried Mr. Randall. 'I didn't think you were coming' he said. 'I'm sorry' I replied, 'I had a hard day at work and dozed off in the chair but I'm alright now.' 'Robbie can't make it' he continued, 'He's got a filthy cold so we've all got to work that little bit harder tonight also he usually comes with me to deliver the barrels on the horse and cart so do you think you could take his place, it'll make you late home. 'That's all right' I replied, thinking I might get a little extra money if I go with him. The boat was late tonight probably because of the strong winds and it was almost half past ten when it came slowly into view by which time we were all thoroughly wet through. I found myself looking towards the cottage that housed the white cat but it was nowhere to be seen. Suddenly the window lit up and there it was, it was time to begin the unloading. It took the craft several minutes to tie up to the pole as the swell kept drifting the boat past it but eventually they succeeded and we entered the water and waded carefully out to it. It was a dangerous job with the boat tossing and turning and we received several knocks from it as it thrashed around madly in the waves. The unloading took longer than usual and we were all relieved when the last barrel was ashore. It had been hard work and we were all exhausted. There were certainly more barrels than usual and I wondered what kind of journey the crew had endured before arriving at Woolverstone, they would certainly enjoy a better journey home wherever that was. Once more the customary glass of rum was offered and it was certainly welcome tonight. Mr. Randall instructed us to load the barrels onto the cart and when it was completed he wished the older man goodnight and passed him ten pounds while asking me to climb aboard and join him on the cart. As we slowly moved forwards I noticed the cat in the window could no longer be seen and the boat had also disappeared from view. I wondered where we were going, I would certainly soon find out. We headed across rough ground towards Pin Mill, eventually pulling up outside the outbuildings in the concrete yard of the Butt and Oyster Public House. A figure appeared out of the darkness and unlocked the door to one of the sheds. ' I wondered where on earth you'd got to,' he moaned, 'You're late tonight.' 'It's this blasted weather' Mr. Randall replied. 'They had a job to get here, one 'R' and one 'W' he continued addressing me. I strained my eyes to read the letters on the barrels and made sure I gave him the correct ones.

I was aware of money changing hands and then it was off again up the road from Pin Mill before turning right down a track to our second delivery place where I spotted a sign saying 'The Riga', it was obviously another Public House where once more we were met by a man almost hidden in wet weather gear. This was followed by a third call at 'The Foresters Arms' on the main road and finally the last two barrels that were to go to 'The Red Lion'. After that, it was time to take the empty cart back and Mr. Randall took a detour so he could go past my cottage and drop me off, something I was grateful for as the night was going fast. Before leaving him I felt I had to know and decided to take a chance. 'What do the letters on the barrels mean?' I asked, 'Does that indicate the different types of oil in them?' He burst out laughing, 'That was just a story' he said, 'It isn't oil at all it's booze. The 'R' is Rum, the 'B' Beer and the 'W' is Whisky. By the way here's your money' with which he passed me twenty pounds, 'You did a damn good job tonight, are you satisfied?' 'Very' I answered, 'Goodnight' It was actually very much morning, and I was very tired. It was nothing to do with me what was in the barrels and I was glad of the extra money even if it did mean late nights. I went to bed at half-past three with barely three hours sleep before it would be time to start another day's work. I hope these nights don't come around too often......

Chapter 4.

Deliveries Increase.

Over the next three months leading up to Christmas, there were more and more deliveries to contend with and we had to handle two or three a week. Also, the number of barrels was increasing and I wondered how on earth the little boat managed to cope with the terrible winds and rain we were getting. Mr. Randall asked us to keep going until the holiday period when there would be no more deliveries for two or three months, so we needed to make the most of things while we could. I had become his regular assistant on the horse and cart and our route now included the Freston Boot. It meant later nights than ever but fortunately, the day work on the farm was getting easier as there was very little to do. It was one Saturday night about the middle of December that we reported for a special delivery due to arrive at midnight.
It was to be a particularly large one

consisting of just about as many barrels as the boat could carry and it would be necessary to make two trips with the horse and cart, no doubt probably keep us busy all night and we were promised a big bonus on completion of the night's work. Once again the weather was foul with even a fall of snow to make things even worse, we would have to be careful when walking in with the barrels not to slip on the Woolverstone Hard as it was called. The wind had almost reached gale force and we feared the boat might well be late if it made it at all. It was almost one o'clock in the morning, we were just thinking about giving up when suddenly the long slender shape of our boat came into view. It was labouring against the conditions plus the number of barrels on the decks were keeping it deep in the water. We waited, while it tied up to the post and finally it was time to begin unloading, we were in for a hard night. We set off into the water with the waves tearing at our boots and prepared to unload our first barrel. It was hazardous and progress was necessarily very slow. The older man was the first to slip over cursing loudly as he fell into the water. It was at that moment that I suddenly realised the white cat was not visible in the cottage window and I wondered if Mr. Randall had noticed it. I was coming ashore

with my second barrel when a shout rang out above the roaring of the wind. 'Everybody stand perfectly still.' The darkness of the night exploded into light from many powerful well-positioned lights and there seemed to be policemen everywhere. All hell broke loose and people seemed to be running everywhere. I suddenly saw a policeman coming towards me. 'Keep still' he ordered but I had no intention of keeping still. As he grabbed my arm, I thrust the barrel I was carrying into his chest.
He dropped the handcuffs he was desperately trying to put on me and with a groan he fell headlong into the waves. I turned around and grabbing the rope off the post I threw myself onto the deck of the boat for all I was worth. The waves were sweeping the boat away and barrels were falling off it as it was tilted at a crazy angle. I felt myself being thrown off and grabbed for anything I could to keep on board. My hands came into contact with the rope with which had been tied up to the pole but because of its length, I fell off the side of the boat and into the raging water. I found myself under the water and was getting plenty of mouthfuls of filthy seawater fearing I would surely drown as I was no swimmer and I had little chance in these conditions anyway.

Just when I felt sure I could not survive, the little boat was thrown sideways onto the mud; suddenly, I was out of the water and face down on horrible clinging mud, but, at least, I would not drown

The two crew members had been unable to save the pitching boat from being swept onto the mud but although their journey was over mine was only just beginning. Exerting all the strength I could muster I levered myself up on my elbows out of the clinging mud and struggled to get to my feet. At one point I was almost down to my waist in it, surely I was not to die in this terrible place but I might well have done so but for my great strength and determination.

Stumbling forwards, freezing cold and wet through I forced my way towards the shore and the safety of the darkness. I could still hear the noise from the Cat house hard area where the police were obviously still rounding up my colleagues and wondered if the policeman I had hit had managed to survive; however, I had no intention of going back to find out. The wicked weather and terrible conditions had swept the boat well down river which was a blessing for me and I set off across the fields for my cottage, my boots full of water, cold, wet and aching all over, bleeding from a collection of cuts and bruises but still free I let myself in and collapsed exhausted on the floor. Tyke was amazed to see my condition and scraping some of the mud off my face I smiled, I was safe at last and it was a comfort to know that my smuggling days were finally over and, at least, I would have earlier nights from now on.

<u>The Permanent Way.</u>

My view of 'The Permanent Way' is life itself. We are all the same yet, all different. We start and end our lives in the same way, it's what happens in between that sets us apart from each other. I have had an exciting life though I sincerely hope it is not likely to end for some time yet as I am still only forty years old and have a wife and family. I think my story is worth listening to but you, the reader must decide if that is the case. Vicky and I have a second child on the way and I presume his or her name will begin with 'B' and I wonder how far we will get through the alphabet as we journey on through life on 'The Permanent Way'.

Len Biddlecombe.

Chapter 1.

War time baby

I was born Brian Andrew Dale, April 1938 at home the second son of George and Daisy. I should have arrived at Colchester Hospital but being wartime and because I was not renowned for having a lot of patience we never made it to the hospital and the midwife delivered me in the back bed oom of our semi-detached house on the B.1352 road in Upper Dovercourt in Essex. Like many other wartime babies it was an achievement to actually be born at all; and where it wasn't a woman's first child people were encouraged to have their children at home if at all possible. My first memories were of my mother and father being very proud to have produced a brother for Adam who was two years my senior.

My father was a fully trained gunnery officer stationed at Parkeston Quay who specialised in defusing German mines and bombs and although it was a very dangerous job he constantly insisted it was quite safe if you treated each device with respect and strictly observed the rules for disarming them. By night he was a member of the Parkeston Quay Gunnery Team whose job it was to monitor German bombers attempting to cross the North Sea and make their way up to London by following the river Stour which brought them immediately over Harwich and Parkeston Quay. About this time, Hitler had produced the V.1 rocket commonly known as the Doodlebug. It was an unmanned bomb set to follow a course and the engine was designed to cut out at a given point when the device would descend and land in London.

Parkeston set up a gun battery together with searchlights and on hearing the siren and the rocket engine they would firstly find it with the searchlight and then destroy it with gunfire. Some did get through but most of them were exploded harmlessly.

Occasionally one would go off course and when that happened you had to listen for the engine to cut out and then it was time to take shelter for it was coming down. Some fell in and around Harwich but generally speaking we were very fortunate and escaped much better than most areas.

Parkeston set up a gun battery together with searchlights and on hearing the siren and the rocket engine they would firstly find it with the searchlight and then destroy it with gunfire. Some did get through but most of them were exploded harmlessly.

Occasionally one would go off course and when that happened you had to listen for the engine to cut out and then it was time to take shelter for it was coming down. Some fell in and around Harwich but generally speaking we were very fortunate and escaped much better than most areas. My mother would take us out into the back garden at night and watch with us as the noise of a rocket engine would fill the air with its drone and then the searchlights would pick it up and several bangs would explode it. Every time this happened we would cheer but when an occasional one managed to get through and the engine stopped mother would rush us indoors to take cover under the big

I couldn't help wondering if it would be much protection if a bomb made a direct hit on our house but, fortunately, we never found out. During the day, my father would hold classes on the Quay to teach new recruits how to disarm German bombs and shells. Generally, they followed a set pattern in which case there was very little risk involved but occasionally something a bit different would turn up and when it did it was a question of moving slowly and taking great care. It was on one such occasion when my father was demonstrating how to disarm a particularly vicious looking specimen that something went wrong. The students were gathered round him in order to follow exactly what he was doing when the device exploded. Half the blast went over his left shoulder and killed a student behind him while the other half of the blast went over his right shoulder and seriously injured another student nearby. By some miracle, my father wasn't seriously injured receiving mainly flash injuries and multiple shock. He was extremely lucky but his face and hands were covered in shrapnel some of which they were unable to remove, these would remain under his skin for the rest of his life and he delighted in showing them off on every chance he had. He remained in the hospital for a couple of days and then had a week off work to recover at home after which it was to be back to the old routine. A few days after returning to work he was cycling home one evening when a single German plane that had probably strayed off course roared up the road behind him. He drove his bicycle straight into a ditch beside the road and lay there in a heap his bicycle on top of him as the plane sprayed the road with bullets. This probably saved his life but as it was he wasn't hurt at all. He was a tough old bird and joked about it afterwards though I got the feeling he must have been pretty scared at the time. What dangerous times these were, it's a miracle any of us survived but somehow we did though the papers every day told us all about the many people who were not so fortunate. There were many tales of heroism in and around Harwich during the war years but generally speaking I felt we were lucky to be placed where we were. There was no particular advantage in attacking Essex especially when the city of London was situated so close to us. Any bombs that fell on us were usually accidental although that didn't make them any more acceptable.

Chapter 2.

Early Schooldays.

At the age of five, I made my entrance at the local Primary School though with the war still going on my appearances were somewhat haphazard. It was nice having Adam to keep an eye on me especially when things got out of hand in the playground. We made friends of two brothers, Steve and Peter Smith who lived not far from us in Upper Dovercourt. They were a bit more daring than we were and soon suggested we joined up with them on a Saturday morning when they walked down to the town to an Amusement shop on the corner near Dovercourt Railway Station. There were several penny machines in there and as the war had quietened down our parents didn't mind us going out to play with them. Steve had found a pin table machine that would pay 3d for three numbers in a line and for four in a line it would pay out one cigarette, probably a Woodbine but, at least, it was a cigarette! 'Try and get the odd

fag out of your dad's pocket' Steven
suggested 'And we will do the same then we
can stop on the river bank at Bathside and
have a smoke.'

I was seven years old when I had my first
cigarette and I felt very big and important.
We also found an old pipe somebody had
discarded beside the railway line and filling
it up with old cigarette ends we picked up
we took turns smoking it. Steven had a box
of matches and he would light it and puff
away at it before passing it round, we all
took turns at smoking it although it tasted
really vile. Goodness knows what germs
were in the bowl of that pipe but it didn't
seem to do us any harm except the first time
I tried it when it made me violently sick but
I couldn't help wondering if it was caused by
the pipe or perhaps the two large ice creams
I had eaten, or perhaps a combination of the
two. Whatever it was to this day I have
never smoked another pipe. About this time,
I had my first brush with death. It was on a
Friday afternoon when Adam and I had just
returned from school. My father had come
home from work early and mother was
cooking and obviously didn't want us under
her feet. 'Come on' Dad said, 'Let's take Rex
for a walk.' Rex was the family dog, a young
Alsatian who always had plenty of energy
and was always looking for ways to expend

it. We set off down the road to the lower fields near Ramsey, a favourite spot of ours when taking the dog for a walk. Rex loved it there and was soon romping around in the undergrowth. It was as we were making our way back across the field that he disturbed a rabbit and proceeded to chase it. 'That rabbit can run fast' I observed, 'That's because it isn't a rabbit' my father said, 'It's a hare, he won't catch that.' However, Rex had other ideas and seemed to be gaining on it when it threw itself into a small stream that ran across the field. It was about eight feet wide and somehow the hare managed to drag itself out the other side. Rex wasn't going to let him get away with that and dived into the water to swim across after him. Then the chase continued with two bedraggled creatures charging across the field heading for the gate and the busy A120 road.

All the calling and shouting was a waste of time as the hare burst through the gate and rushed across the road. How on earth it managed to miss the wheels of a large lorry making its way to Harwich I will never know but Rex in hot pursuit was not so lucky. He was hit a glancing blow by the wheels of the lorry and by the time we arrived on the scene he was laying on the side of the road. I was screaming surely Rex was dead. The lorry didn't stop though he might have thought he missed the dog. Much to our surprise Rex didn't seem too badly hurt, he was bleeding from the mouth but his legs weren't broken though he did look a sorry state especially being wet through, this made him seem such a poor skinny thing. He seemed to be able to walk alright so Father put him on the lead and we set off slowly to get him home where we could have a better look at him. He polished off some food in his dish and gratefully drank a large amount of water before settling down in his basket. 'Shouldn't we call the vet' I asked. 'No' my father replied, 'We'll see how he is in the morning.' Rex's bed was in the bedroom Adam and I shared and I couldn't help worrying as we tried to get to sleep. He kept on moaning and whimpering and it was difficult to know if he was in pain or dreaming of chasing that hare. I awoke first in the morning and immediately looked across at Rex's bed but he wasn't there. Perhaps he had got up and gone downstairs to get his breakfast. 'Mum' I called, 'How's Rex?' 'I'm sorry Brian' she replied 'He passed away in the night, he must have had serious internal injuries far worse than we thought.' I burst into tears, 'We should have called the vet' I cried, 'He could have saved him' 'He probably couldn't' my father said joining my mother,

'Don't worry, we'll get you another dog'
'But another dog won't be Rex' I yelled. By
now Adam had woken up and gathered what
had happened. We both loved Rex very
much and we threw our arms round each
other and cried bitterly, it was a very
difficult lesson to learn.

Chapter 3.

Peacetime.

It was a time of great celebration in 1945 when the war officially ended. I was nearing my eighth birthday and street parties were the order of the day. Adam and I loved them, waving flags and eating cakes with so many games to play and everybody happy. We were spending more time with Steve and Peter Smith and had branched out a bit, finding our way along the riverside to Bathside and on to Harwich where we discovered Ha'Penny Pier a small pier mainly frequented by fishermen. We were fascinated and decided to make up our own tackle and try our luck. We managed to make up hand lines and Steve and Peter had an older brother who had some fishing tackle with spare hooks and weights. The main problem was what to use for bait but we solved this by putting pieces of bread on the hooks while occasionally we would catch a small crab which we could use. The only thing we didn't catch was any fish! One Sunday afternoon we were fishing in the warm sunshine when we saw some other fishermen on the pier who seemed to be doing quite well. 'What are you using for bait?' I asked, 'Lugworm' came the reply, 'We dug it up this morning. We're going shortly and we've got some worms left over you can have them if you like.' 'Thanks' I replied. We were very excited and couldn't wait for them to pack up their tackle and leave. They eventually pulled their lines in and prepared to go it was our turn now. The worms they gave us were not much good, just bits and pieces really and they were difficult to thread on the hooks but we didn't care, we were real fishermen now.

We tried and tried, unsuccessfully to catch something but to no avail and eventually we had to reluctantly admit defeat as it was time to go and anyway we were running out of bait fast. Suddenly Adam's line started going mad pulling away from us, going this way and that in the water defying all our efforts to pull it in. Fortunately, another fisherman on the pier came to our rescue. Realising we were in trouble he took over and hauled the line onto the pier. The result was staggering, on the end of it was a great big round fish about the size of a large dinner plate with two enormous wings and a tail covered in

scales and a spike, we had never seen
anything like it. 'What is it?' I asked, 'It's a
skate' the fisherman answered, 'Well done,
that's worth a bob or two' The whole thing
frightened the life out of us but somehow we
had to get the hook out of its mouth for we
were not going home now, we were going to
fish some more. Adam turned the fish on it's
back and put his foot on it to hold it still
while he took the hook out of the mouth.
Suddenly the fish wrapped it's wings round
Adam's foot and he couldn't get it out. The
man tried to help us rescue his foot but the
fish was not impressed and with a swish of
its tail it slashed into Adam's Wellington
boot splitting it from top to bottom. Going
by the screams Adam was making it would
seem his leg may be cut as well. We rescued
his foot and took off what was left of his
boot and sock to find a long deep gash on
his leg that was bleeding freely. One of the
fishermen went off to call an ambulance
while another wrapped a cloth around his
leg to try to stem the flow of blood
Goodness knows what that cloth had
contained though it didn't look very clean, I
wondered if it had contained their worms, I
must say it made me feel very sick.
The ambulance quickly turned up and
carried all four of us boys off to the hospital
where Adam had a couple of stitches and a

tetanus injection to make sure he would suffer no ill effects after which our parents were contacted and my father and Mr. Smith turned up in his old Morris to collect us and take us home. Needless to say, we were not very popular and we had to promise our fishing days were well and truly over, we would have to find some other form of entertainment. Mr Smith promised us he would take us all fishing one of these days though I certainly don't remember him ever doing so. It wasn't till we got back home that our father asked us exactly what happened. 'Adam caught a big skate' I explained 'But when he put his foot on it to try to get the hook out of its mouth it wrapped it's wings round his foot and he couldn't get it out. We managed to get his foot out but then the fish flashed it's tail with the big spike on it and tore his Wellington boot to pieces.' 'It must have been a big fish' my father said, 'What happened to it ?' For the first time we looked at each other, none of us had any idea. 'The other fisherman probably kept it' I answered, at which we all burst out laughing. We would not be going to the Ha'Penny pier anymore, at least not to do any fishing. At our young age, it was far too dangerous and we had received a severe warning. Perhaps when we were older we might try our luck at fishing again but for the moment, it was better we leave it to the more experienced people. We would always enjoy watching them and perhaps learning something and who knows, one day we may even be the 'fishermen' that other young boys may come to watch.

Chapter 4.

Learning to Swim

I was barely nine years old when the time came for Adam to leave our Primary School and go to the Secondary Modern in Manningtree It was a nasty shock to find out he wasn't there to watch over me. Steven Smith also left at the same time and Peter and I were left on our own. We developed a very close friendship and he was determined to teach me to swim. 'Most important thing in the world' he said, 'Especially if you are going to get a job on one of the North Sea ferries.' At that time, I had made up my mind to go for such a job and I had told him of my intentions. We did go once a week to a local swimming pool with the school but only to splash about in the shallow end. Peter had learnt to swim very early in life and promised to help me. 'We'll go to the Ha'Penny pier' he said 'One Saturday afternoon when the tide is about three o'clock.' I admit I was very frightened by the idea but it was so important and I felt I could trust him

Meanwhile, I had fallen out with my father as he and my mother argued over whether or not to have another dog. My mother was all for the idea but my father was adamant. 'No' he firmly stated, 'It's too upsetting when you lose them. Vet bills are so damned high we just can't afford it anyway.' There was no way of persuading him and I decided I didn't love him anymore so I wouldn't tell him about our swimming plans. One Saturday in early summer Peter informed me that the tide was just about right for our first swimming lesson and we walked down to Dovercourt Station and then on the sea wall along Bathside to Harwich. There were very few people about with one solitary fisherman on the pier. We had our swimming trunks on under our trousers and together we stripped off. The sight of the water frightened the life out of me. 'How deep is it here' I asked, 'No depth at all' Peter assured me, 'Watch' with that he waded in and started swimming. 'Come on' he yelled and convinced that it was shallow I waded into the water. It was very cold. 'It's O.K. once you get under' Peter declared and with that I squatted down in the water and found that he was right. 'Now take your feet off the bottom and swim with me' he called. I don't quite know what happened next, one minute I was doing a sort of dogs paddle the next I seemed to lose my confidence and fell over onto my back. I must have panicked and swallowed gallons of water before attempting to regain my footing on the bottom, but to my horror it wasn't there, I was out of my depth and drowning fast. Added to that I bashed my head on one of the shell encrusted legs of the pier and lost consciousness. I was going to drown the very first time I had been in the water.

I came to in a bed with a pipe attached to me laying on my stomach spitting out horrible tasting seawater with a worried looking Peter sitting beside me. 'Where am I?' I gasped. 'You're in hospital' Peter replied 'I thought you were drowning, some man dived in and rescued you.' 'I think I've swallowed half the river' I said. 'Your father is on his way' Peter declared just to make me feel ten times worse. Fifteen minutes later he arrived and to my surprise was most understanding. 'What on earth were you doing?' he asked, 'That isn't a safe place to learn to swim, the current there is far too dangerous and there are so many obstacles about under the water, if you want to learn to swim then I'll take you to a swimming pool and teach you myself.' And so he did. My love for my father had returned and by the time I was ten years old I could swim or,

at least, support myself in the water though I wouldn't fancy my chances in the North Sea.
My attention returned to my family and I asked my mother why my brother's name began with an 'A' and mine with a 'B'.
'I'm learning the alphabet at school' I said, 'Will our next babies name begin with a 'C' ?'
'There'll be no more babies' my mother declared, 'The subject is closed.' Although it meant nothing to me at the time, years later I discovered that while Adam had been a normal birth mine had been anything but normal and afterwards it became necessary for my mother to have a hysterectomy, there would certainly be no more babies.
I decided the time had come for me to drop my middle name in order to get rid of my initials B.A.D. which some of my schoolmates thought was most appropriate. Why my parents saddled me with those initials I had no idea. I decided it was probably accidental and was ready to give them the benefit of the doubt though I am sure there must be other people who have been given names and initials they may have had cause to regret.
I wondered if my mother and father had given me those initials deliberately or whether they didn't realise how I would suffer as a result of it. Either way I vowed

that when it was my turn to think of initials for my children I would be more careful.

Chapter 5.

Trouble at Sea.

I liked being on the water much more than under it and Adam and me together with Steven and Peter often went to Ha'Penny Pier to catch the British Rail ferries to Felixstowe and Shotley. There were three boats operating the trips, two identical sister ships the Epping and Hainault, one covered the Harwich to Shotley run while the other was used as a spare to cover the journeys. The more turbulent route from Harwich to Felixstowe was in the hands of the M.V. Brightlingsea which was a much larger boat. There was not much to see at Shotley though the pier was much longer than the one at Harwich and there was usually a number of fishermen on it. A funny thing happened there one Sunday afternoon. We had just landed and stopped to watch the fishermen. One of them had caught a large flatfish I later learned was a plaice and he was proudly showing it off by laying it on a sack near the side of the pier for everybody to see. We stood looking at it and I realised the poor thing was dying. It was opening and closing its gills and seemed to be struggling more and more to breathe. 'It's suffering' I told Adam and worked my way nearer to it. I couldn't bear to see it and with a deft flick of my right foot, I kicked it back over the side and into the water. The man went mad. I ran for all I was worth, down the pier with the man close behind me.

By the time we reached the end of the pier he had finally caught up with me and grabbed me from behind knocking me over. Another man on the pier grabbed the fisherman and demanded to know what on earth he was doing.

'He knocked my beautiful fish back into the water' came the reply, 'Well you can't manhandle him like that, take his name and address and call and see the village policeman, he'll go and see his father and he'll sort it out.' 'What's your name and address' the man demanded, I had to think fast. 'John Osborne' I announced, '15, Main Road Shotley, please don't tell the policeman, he'll call on my father and I'll get a good hiding.' 'And so you should' the fisherman said, 'That's the best fish I've caught for ages.'

We had to get back to Harwich as soon as

we could and we decided to stay away from
Shotley for a while. I preferred the run to
Felixstowe, it was usually a bit choppy
cutting across the river and when we docked
near Marriages Mill we had to jump on to a
floating pontoon which could be a bit
exciting if the weather was bad. I also
enjoyed the visit we always made to Butlin's
Amusement Park. Another enjoyable
Saturday outing was to go with our fathers
down the road to the Royal Oak Public
House while they enjoyed a pint inside we
sat outside with a lemonade and a bag of
crisps before crossing the road and going
into the ground of Harwich and Parkeston
Football Club. Wearing our black and white
scarves and rosettes we would join the
hundred or so supporters that regularly
turned up to follow the Shrimpers as they
were called. Our greatest thrill was when
they played in the Amateur Cup although
they normally got beaten we loved it. Their
crowning glory came in 1953 when they
won their way through all the rounds to
reach the final at Wembley. We got tickets
and joined all the supporters on the many
coaches, it was a great day out and we loved
every minute, the only thing to spoil the day
was the result, Pegasus beat us 6-0! Shortly
after my fifteenth birthday, we received a
phone call one evening asking my father to

go into work. A Dutch ferry, the Kronprins Frederick had caught fire while tied up at Parkeston Quay. The fire was so intense the Port Authority decided to cast her off and allow the fire to burn itself out. All the passengers were safe and she eventually turned over onto her side. She remained there for a couple of months or more before being righted and towed to Belgium for repair. While she was there another ship, the British Rail ferry Duke of York was involved in a collision in the North Sea and her bow section right up to the bridge was ripped off and sank. She was towed into Parkeston Quay and tied up beside the 'Frederick.' Local papers showed photographs of the two under the heading 'A graveyard for ships.' My father took us all down to see it and I think it was this that finally convinced me to forget about a career afloat.

I decided instead I would be the next centre forward for Harwich and Parkeston and take them to Wembley again, this time, we would win that cup. Around my sixteenth birthday, I duly signed on for Lawford Lads football club in the Essex Border League. Adam had left school and been called up for two years National Service in the Army. I well remember the day he said his farewells and clutching his travel warrant in his hand he left for the railway station. Meanwhile, I had a severe setback to my plans when I was seriously hurt in a tackle by an over- zealous defender. It was a serious knee injury and I left the ground on crutches. It was back to the hospital again to hear the news that this was ultimately the premature end to my football career at the tender age of seventeen. I took a job locally in a furniture shop to carry me through to the time when I would have to go away for my own National Service. The pay was poor but at least, it was a job.

Chapter 6.

National Service.

I was seventeen and a half when I
received my call-up papers.
Conscription was still in force and I
would have to go in either the Army or the
R.A.F. for two years service. I chose the
latter though goodness knows why perhaps
it was because I felt it was the lesser of two
evils. It was my turn to go out into the wide
world now and I left just before my
eighteenth birthday to travel to the receiving
station at Cardington in Bedfordshire.
There we underwent medical examinations,
received various injections and took a short
arms parade. For anyone that hasn't heard of
that one before we all stripped off and stood
in lines. Doctors came round examining us
for any trace of Venereal Disease, quite an
eye opener that was. I think about 99% of us

passed that examination, I wondered how many would have passed it if they gave it to us at the end of our service. I served my drill period, square bashing as it was known at R.A.F. West Kirby on the Wirral for eight weeks after which it was 'trade' training at R.A.F. Hereford for six weeks before being given my first permanent posting. I was to be a wages clerk and was posted to a station near Bristol where I spent all my time. There were about 250 young men there and 30 young women. As you could imagine the women were in great demand though they always seemed to cope. I was not one of the great lovers flexing their muscles but preferred instead to spend my time at the village pub. Scrumpy Cider was very popular mainly because it was 7d. Pint and with little money it was the perfect beverage. It was horrible, made from rotten apples it tasted like it and reminded me of engine oil. Nevertheless, I became quite used to it and could put away quite a bit. One night I had been drinking heavily with two other lads, we set off for the camp on our bicycles.

We travelled round the perimeter track and down the runway in the darkness and were having a race to see who could get back first. I was in the lead when I hit one of the landing lights and was catapulted over the handlebars on to the concrete runway. I suffered several cuts and bruises and was knocked out but luckily the lads got me back to the camp and took me to the station sick quarters where they kept me in overnight. When I awoke in the morning it was to see the medical officer looking at my chart on the rail at the bottom of my bed. 'You are a fool laddie' he said, 'You have alcoholic poisoning, give it up or it will give you up.' It frightened the life out of me and to this day I haven't been able to face a glass of cider, in fact for a long time I couldn't even face a glass of anything. It was on one of my weekend visits home that I learned that my father had no longer been required to work at Parkeston Quay, in peacetime they were laying several workers off. He was fortunate to get a job with British Rail driving freight and passenger trains from Parkeston Station. My mother's health had deteriorated and she was struggling to manage the house at the age of 50! My father was spending more and more time away and this was making life intolerable for my mother. Fortunately, Adam had completed his service in the Army but he made it clear that he was going to try to get a job in London as the wages were much better there. In September, the weather took a turn for the worse and strong winds and snow showers were the order of the day. This meant my father being away more than ever as he was often stranded in another part of the country. Everything came to a head in October when my mother suffered a bad fall in the garden and ended up in a hospital with a broken hip. It was the beginning of the end for her and she never really recovered dying a month later. Before leaving for my National Service I had started up a friendship with Vicky, a young girl who lived in West Street in Harwich. We had been to school together and I always fancied her. She was an only child and her father had left her mother some time before. Whenever I was home I used to do what I could to help her and after my mother died I spent more time at Vicky's than at home. I promised myself that when I was demobbed I would ask her to marry me. It transpired that my father had found consolation with another woman who he had spent time with while he was away overnight. He told me he intended to move in with her and he would leave our house in Dovercourt jointly to Adam and me, we could sell it and share the money. Adam had succeeded in getting a job in London with an advertising company and was living in a flat in the city.

He wrote to me saying he had found love with a local girl there and was not coming back to Dovercourt to live, perhaps I could buy his share of the house but I was unable to do so.

My demob date arrived and after getting home my first job was to ask Vicky to marry me and she duly accepted. In our early twenties, we were married in the local church and moved into my old house to live. With her mother's help, I was able to get a mortgage and pay Adam his half share of the value of the house. Very soon after this Vicky told me we were going to start a family and I would need to get a job. Meanwhile, her mum was happy to return my help by keeping us going financially.

<u>Chapter 7.</u>

A Bolt from the Blue.

Vicky was having a fairly quiet pregnancy and with her mum's help, she was coping well. I was able to be a husband and a son while searching for a job of some sort. It was just after my birthday in April that we had a surprise visitor one evening. There was a knock at the door and who should be there but my brother Adam. He was delighted to see me and meet Vicky for the first time. We had so much to talk about we stayed up for most of the night. He had no intention of ever coming back to Dovercourt to live and had been told by his company that they were anxious to open up a business in Germany where they felt there was massive scope for advertising. They wanted him to take over the challenge and move there to live. He was happy to do this and knowing I had just left the forces he suggested they could do worse than to give me an interview for his old job in London. 'I am sure you could do it' he said 'And they have agreed to meet you.' 'I wouldn't live in London' I declared, 'My life is here with Vicky and our family.' 'Would you be prepared to travel backwards and forwards every day?' Adam asked, 'If it was worthwhile' I replied. The rest of the night was spent discussing all the details of the job and I really began to fancy it. 'This is peacetime' Adam said, 'Companies are beginning to wake up, you could be on a good thing. With regard to travelling, with Felixstowe Docks increasing their container traffic and Townsend Thoresen operating three North Sea crossings every day to Zeebrugge, Harwich are losing out on daily passenger trips to the Hook of Holland and are going to concentrate on freight boats and enticing liners to use the port for collecting and returning passengers for foreign cruises, I was reading all about it in the paper the other day.

To do this they must improve the rail link to London, and with the commuter trade going through the roof they are going to kill two birds with one stone, by increasing the size of the early morning train. 'The Boat Train' as it's called leaving here at 7am to reach

Liverpool Street by 9am, returning at 5 o'clock which would get you home by 7 pm. You'd be able to get a season ticket from Monday to Friday which the company would pay for. You can't lose as long as you don't find the travailing too much for you.' I said this didn't worry me and the London wages would be just what we needed with a family on the way. Adam promised to get on to his company and iron out the details but there wasn't likely to be a problem.

It seemed the answer to our prayers if it came off and I went to bed much happier than I had been for a long time. Next morning he was on his way promising to get in touch with his company that very day. Two days later a letter arrived from Collins and Company asking me to attend at their London office for an interview a few days later. I travelled to the city and found the London office without much trouble as it was situated near Liverpool Street Station. After a long day and an extensive interview, I was on my way back to Harwich as an advertising officer with Adam's company.

The deal was most acceptable, an excellent rate of pay, plus commission and generous expenses, including the railway season ticket with a starting date the following Monday morning. Vicky was a little concerned that my days away from her would be long but to have Saturday and Sunday off would be a wonderful bonus.

I went to the railway station and enquired about the Boat Train, confirming it departed every morning at 7am and after calling at Colchester and Chelmsford it was scheduled to arrive at Liverpool Street at 8.45am. The return left at 5pm meaning I would be back home by 7 o'clock. It was agreed that Vicky's mum would move in with us, after all, we had plenty of room, this would enable Vicky to help her and in return, she could keep an eye on her daughter and help her if the baby should come while I was away . Arrangements were in hand for the baby to be born in Colchester General Hospital and as a safeguard, I put a local taxi firm on standby to take them if anything happened while I wasn't

there, a simple phone call and they would be on their way. I was still without transport and had arranged to have driving lessons at the weekends after settling into my new job and hoped to pass my driving test fairly quickly so we could get a little car.

The last weekend before I was to start my job I decided to devote entirely to being with my wife.

On Saturday I took her shopping in Colchester followed by a slap up meal, then

on Sunday morning, we took a quiet stroll along the beach at Dovercourt Bay while in the afternoon we went to the cinema and watched a film, something we hadn't done since we married. Vicky's mum decided to let us spend the entire
weekend together and stayed out of the way at home. She said she wanted to do some baking but I had a feeling she was being diplomatic and leaving us on our own. Vicky was getting big now and was feeling rather uncomfortable but she thoroughly enjoyed our time together.
Eventually, the Monday morning dawned and I left home at 6.30am to walk down to Parkeston Station to begin my first journey to London.

Chapter 8.

The Boat Train.

Arriving at Parkeston Quay Station in good time I was faced by a long train waiting to leave for London. It was like a great big silver snake and was fully twelve carriages in length. 'Please board the front eight carriages for Liverpool Street' the Stationmaster said, 'The rear four carriages will be dropped at Colchester and become the 8.15 to Ipswich.' I settled down in the forward carriages and opened the morning paper I'd just purchased on the station. It was announced that a Restaurant car was available on the train and I decided I would attend and eat a hearty breakfast in case I didn't get any lunch. I anticipated enjoying a late tea at home when I got back with some of mother-in-law's delicious cake to follow. At exactly seven o'clock we began our journey. The carriages were almost full and were obviously containing city businessmen. Slowly we crept along the dock passing the oil tanks before turning to the left and rising up the gradient, then a sharp right hand turn and we were entering the wooded area that stretched most of the

way to Wrabness Station. I struck up a conversation with another smartly suited passenger who had obviously become a regular traveller. 'We pass another train in a couple of minutes' he said , 'We call it the 'little fella' it's just two carriages and has come from Manningtree to call at Parkeston Quay before going on to Harwich Town. They call this the Mayflower Line because of its scenic route and views across the river. Sorry,' he said 'I do ramble on a bit' 'Most interesting,' I replied. Moments later the 'little fella' rattled past us and looking at his watch my companion observed that it was bang on time. 'I' m Ray by the way' he said offering his hand 'Brian' I replied shaking it warmly, 'This is my very first day.' 'I normally go to breakfast now' he observed, 'Will you join me?' 'Yes' I said, 'What's it like' 'Nothing special'
he replied 'And bloody expensive but it's hot, and we need something.'
It was as he said 'bloody expensive' but the breakfast itself wasn't bad, Egg, Bacon, Sausage, Tomatoes and Beans with toast washed down with coffee. I must confess I felt much better afterwards, the only trouble was the train had picked up speed and I found it difficult to eat and drink coffee with the constant swaying. Ray laughed, 'You'll get used to it' he stated, 'It comes with

practice. There was a large crowd in the Restaurant car and I observed that British Rail
was making a good profit what with the fares and returns from the Restaurant car, 'There's no competition' Ray replied, 'We have to leave home so early we don't have time for breakfast, do you drive?' 'I'm going to take lessons' I replied,
'My wife's pregnant, first one.' 'Where do you live?' he asked, 'High Road Dovercourt' I answered, 'So do I' Ray said, 'When we get back tonight I'll give you a lift home, maybe I can give you the odd lesson or two next weekend' 'That would be great' I answered smiling, I'd made a good friend on my first day. The train lumbered on gradually slowing down to stop at Colchester, a few minutes to unhook the rear four carriages and we wee off again. Ray and I left the Restaurant car and wandered back to our seats feeling more like facing the new day. After a quick call at Chelmsford we were off again and very soon we were slowing down to pull into Liverpool Street Station dead on time at 8.45am.
There was a mad rush down the platform and Ray and I got split up in the crowd. I knew it was only a very short walk to Collins & Company the advertising firm I had joined and found it with ease. It was

exactly 9 o'clock when I entered the offices to be greeted with a warm handshake by a gentleman who introduced himself as George Collins, one of the executive partners. I hadn't seen him when I came for my interview and wondered where the other two gentlemen I remembered from my last visit were today. I was shown into the back office where I would be working and introduced to the staff. They were a bit of a mixed bunch, my immediate boss, Chris Day was an elderly man
probably in his late fifties while my associate officer, Bob Williams was probably in his late thirties and then there was the secretary Rita Oliver, she was young, about twenty, very attractive with a charming smile, I felt I was going to enjoy working here. Over the next few days, I was given a complete rundown on the firm's operations and met several people connected to various Radio Stations and Newspapers. Advertising was big business and the work very challenging and competitive but great fun. 'We need to outwit our opponents with clever slogans that sell products' Mr. Collins explained, 'I don't expect you to come up with too many slogans to start with but I'm sure you'll learn as we go along.' 'I'll do my best Sir' I answered,
'We'll soon knock you into shape' Chris said

and I was fairly sure they would.

My friendship with Ray was a blessing. He regularly picked me up in the morning and dropped me off at home in the evening. He gave me an hour's lesson at the weekend and in return we had him and his wife Betty round for a meal at our house and soon we were interchanging, going for a meal one Saturday night at his house and the next at ours.

Chapter 9.

A Dangerous Game.

It was after I had completed my first month in the city and received my first wages cheque and expenses payment that Chris Day called me into his office one Monday morning. 'We've been invited to discuss an advertising campaign with a company in Bristol' he said, 'It's for one of their products, a washing powder. Somebody will have to go there and it will mean stopping at a hotel for a couple of nights while filming takes place. Normally I would send Bob to do it but he is away on location in Wales would you be prepared to have a go at it?' 'Of course' I replied confidently, 'When would I need to go?' 'Tomorrow if you can,' he said, 'I'll need to pack a bag' I replied, 'Otherwise there's no problem' 'Rita will go with you' Chris Day announced , 'She'll be a great help, I'll arrange two train tickets and book two rooms at the Great Western Hotel for two nights you can pay for your meals yourselves and claim the money back when you return.' 'Right Sir' I said pleased that he felt I could manage it and having Rita there wit her experience would be a great help. I arrived at work on Tuesday morning, with my small case containing a change of clothes and after a last briefing, it was time to go with Rita to the underground station. We travelled across London to Paddington Station to catch the 11am train to Bristol. Rita was great company, bubbling with excitement. It was easy to see why she was in advertising and I had a feeling she would be instrumental in finding the necessary slogans to satisfy our contractors. On the way to Bristol, she told me all about her young life. She was 23 years old and lived with her parents on the outskirts of London. She joined Collins and Company about twelve months before I did and had been instrumental in helping them to land several contracts although her job was actually on the secretarial side. She hadn't got a boyfriend and wasn't particularly interested in getting one preferring to play the field and have a good time. She was still young enough to enjoy life without getting tied down. I was enjoying the journey remembering the many times I had made it before while I was in the forces.

We arrived at Temple Mead Station just before 5 o'clock after making several stops on the way.

While stationed near Bristol on my National Service I had visited the city several times and wondered if I could remember anything about it, certainly I remembered seeing the Great Western Hotel though I'd never stayed there. We took a taxi from the station and were soon checking in. Two rooms had been booked for us and they were apparently numbers 18 and 19 on the first floor. 'I'll take this one' Rita said as we entered the first of the two rooms. They were very basic with a three-quarter bed, en-suite facilities, washbasin and television set. I was left with number 19 next door which was a carbon copy of the other one. There was time for a quick shower and change of clothes but I was still in my pants when a knock at the door preceded Rita's urgent voice. 'Ready for tea?' she asked, I opened the door and she breezed in. Suddenly I realised I was only in my 'Y' fronts and she had obviously noticed this. 'Well' she began, 'We do make a sight for sore eyes don't we' I felt embarrassed, 'Sorry' I began realising how pathetic the remark sounded, 'I didn't wish to show myself off' She laughed, 'Don't be sorry' she said, 'It's the best sight I've seen all day' I began to realise I was playing a dangerous game and ignoring the remark I put my shirt on and slipped into my trousers. I had to admit I fancied her, who wouldn't but I had to remember that I was married, deeply in love with Vicky and about to become a father. 'Let's go to tea' I suggested slipping on my jacket and shoes. Her eyes sparkled cheekily and slipping her arm in mine we made for the stairs. 'Let's have a drink first' she said 'After all it is still a bit early, perhaps after tea we can have a quick look round Bristol, we might as well enjoy ourselves while we can.' I agreed, there was no harm in it as long as I watched things very carefully. I felt as though I could easily get drawn into something I would regret. With that, we went downstairs to the bar. I was a little surprised to find Rita was a wine drinker and a heavy one at that. I was quite satisfied with a couple of pints of beer but she quickly disposed of a bottle of red and was looking for a glass of the house wine with her meal. The tea itself was very simple and I paid for it and got a receipt. I would claim it back on expenses when we returned to London, with regard to the bottle of wine that would have to depend on the success of our business tomorrow. 'Let's go to a cinema' Rita suggested after we had finished our tea and we did. I was careful not to attempt to put my arm around her and, to be honest, she seemed to understand. I had already told her my situation at home on the train journey down to Bristol and she obviously accepted I would not try anything. After the film we made our way back to the hotel, I put a call through to Vicky to confirm everything was alright and after a nightcap in the bar we made our way to our rooms, I was feeling very tired, I wasn't used to bars, restaurants or cinemas but I got the impression that she was.

Chapter 10.

Busy day and a Boozy night!.

I settled down in my easy chair and switched on the television. After hearing the local news I dozed off and woke up with a start. It was after midnight and the television had finished it's programmes for the night so I switched it off, put the light off and got into bed. I had no trouble going back to sleep and it must have been around 2 o'clock when I awoke with a start. I am a very light sleeper and realised at once that somebody had tried to open my door. Fortunately I had locked it and I had a good idea who was on the other side of it. I laid still in the darkness for a few minutes but they didn't try it anymore so I decided to turn over and go back to sleep. I woke up at half past six with the spring sunshine streaming through my window. I was used to rising early and was soon enjoying a shower and a shave before dressing. I couldn't help wondering how the day would go and was barely finishing dressing when Rita knocked on my door. I was at least fully decent when I let her in and she asked me how I had slept. I didn't mention the person who tried my door thinking it was better forgotten. We went down to breakfast after which it was time to set off for I.T.V. South West to meet our customer. The product we were required to produce a slogan and advertising programme for was a new washing powder called Daisy Fresh incorporating a stain remover. Rita immediately came up with the slogan that it would grow on you and I suggested it would clean your clothes while it refreshed your nose, we had made a start. Rita was brilliant and I felt she could have handled the project on her own. The whole thing was recorded and completed by lunchtime and we were treated to a good meal before moving on to South Wales and the West Television Studios to start all over again. When we finally finished filming it was late afternoon. I decided to put through a quick telephone call to Vicky to make sure all was well and received some amazing news. She had been rushed into Colchester General Hospital during the early hours of the morning and had just given birth to a baby boy. Mother and son were both doing well and mother-in-law said they hadn't been able to contact me but there was absolutely no need to worry as everything had gone off perfectly and Vicky was sleeping peacefully.

It was a blessing that her mother had been with her. I was a father, what a wonderful surprise. Rita threw her arms around me and shouted 'Congratulations, this calls for a celebration' and celebrate we certainly did. Back at the hotel we tackled a couple of bottles of wine after a toast with Champagne. Ten o'clock saw us still drinking as we relaxed in her room. We were going to return to London the next day having clinched the deal with Daisy Fresh Washing Powder and that was an added reason to celebrate. I was feeling very drunk and was having a job to stay awake. 'You were brilliant Brian' she said, 'You're going to be a big success in this job I feel sure.' She seemed to be handling things very well and rang for some more wine to be sent up. I don't remember much after that, I think I was sick but everything was very blurred. I woke up and looking at my watch I found it was after two in the morning. I had a blinding headache and was in her bed, the trouble was she was in it with me and we were both naked. The room was a bit of a mess. It was obvious we had attempted to have sex though in my state I was doubtful if it had been successful. I hated myself for what I had done, there was poor Vicky in hospital recovering from her ordeal and how I'd let her down, I didn't deserve her and I was deeply ashamed. Rita was fast asleep and not trusting myself to walk back to my room I turned over and went back to sleep slipping on my pants first in a pathetic gesture to make everything right, I do believe I was quietly crying. We quickly finished off our business with the Daisy Fresh company and clutching our signed contract we were ready to return to London by lunchtime. Rita hadn't mentioned the previous night and neither had I, whatever happened it was better forgotten for we both knew there was no possible future in it and I felt we would never be able to work together on location again. Bob Williams would have to work with Rita and I would have to tackle lesser tasks on my own. Bob would be a much better prospect for her anyway, though in his late thirties he was separated from his wife who had left him for another man. They had not had a family so there was nothing to hold him back. I pointed this out to Rita on the train journey back to London and she agreed. 'I'm sorry about last night' she said, 'So am I but it's over and we can't change it' I replied, 'It must be forgotten, I don't blame you, after all we are both adults and we were very much the worse for drink I just feel terrible because my wife Vicky had been going through her ordeal and I wasn't there with her, she would have expected a lot more from me and I feel ashamed that I let her down so badly.' The train was arriving at Paddington now and she gave me a knowing look. 'Oh well' she said, 'Back to work let's go and get the congratulations we deserve.'

Chapter 11.

A Terrible Accident.

The next three months passed without any further problems with Vicky and her mother looking after Ashley and my work progressing normally. I had not been away with Rita anymore and our friendship with Ray and his wife Betty at home flourished. He gave me a number of driving lessons and I took my test and passed first time. We spent each Saturday evening with them, one week at our house and the next at theirs enjoying a meal and a bottle of wine. It was around the middle of October when the weather began to change. The Summer had given way to a brief Autumn and suddenly we were in the depths of Winter. It was much colder and we were getting an enormous amount of rain, added to this the wind had increased to near gale force and was continuing day after day. The East Coast was under flood alert and there were days when we were unable to go to work because it was considered too dangerous to run the Boat Train. The line from Parkeston to Manningtree passed through heavy woodland and with the ground so waterlogged and the wind so strong there was a danger of trees falling and it was considered too dangerous to use the line. At times like that buses would replace the train but they were so slow, overcrowded and meant arriving so late in London we found it wasn't worth bothering. Chris Day was a very understanding employer and left the decision to me but Ray's boss was more demanding and he was worried that he might have to move to London or he might lose his job. One Monday morning he picked me up as usual and we drove down to Parkeston Quay. I had been looking at cars all weekend without making any decision, I think I wanted something really good for a pittance and it was proving hard to find. It had been raining hard all night and the wind had reached gale force by the time we arrived at the Quay. 'Is the train running?' Ray asked, 'It is at the moment' came the reply 'Though I don't know if it will get you back tonight.' We decided we had to go in and we'd worry about getting back later. The train pulled out as usual at 7am, you could set your watch by it. Was it our imagination or was it going slower than usual. Along the Quay we went, past the Oil Refinery and the fuel storage tanks although they were hard to see in the gathering gloom partly caused by the weather and partly by the darker mornings we were going to have to get used to. We sensed the normal sweeping left turn and rise of the gradient, I'd got used to it by now and could tell where we were by the movement of the carriages. 'Breakfast?' Ray asked, 'O.K.' I replied and we moved off in the direction of the Restaurant car. When we got there I noticed a worried look on Ray's face.

'What's wrong?' I asked, 'Come without your wallet?' 'No' Ray replied, 'Something's not quite right.' 'What do you mean?' I asked, 'We haven't passed the 'little fella' we should have done so by now.' It was still dark but Ray knew we should have seen the lights of the little train as it passed us, and it should have done so before now. 'Maybe it's running late' I said, 'It's never late' Ray replied. We were gathering speed now and rattling along much more normally. We were midway between Parkeston Quay and Wrabness Station in the thickest part of the wooded area when it happened. Screeching brakes suddenly filled the air, the train lurched wickedly to the right and there was an almighty crash. All the lights went out and we were covered by shattered glass and broken wood and metal while plates and dishes were flying everywhere. People were screaming and the whole carriage was a mass of hissing steam. Human bodies were flying all over the place, added to the fact that we were in total darkness it made the whole thing hideous. Everything was at a standstill now and there was an eerie silence broken only by the moans and screams of people obviously in pain trapped beneath amounts of rubble. I had no idea where Ray had gone but I had to lever myself up on one elbow to see if I could stand up and was surprised to find I didn't appear to be too badly hurt. My face was covered in blood with several deep gashes bleeding freely but I didn't appear to have any broken bones, certainly my legs and arms felt as though they were alright although they were aching . I struggled to my feet and cursed as I cut my leg on a large bit of broken glass from the window which had been completely shattered. The train had obviously crashed but into what? 'Is everybody alright?' I shouted and received a mixed response. I wondered how many people were unable to reply. One of the restaurant staff produced a torch and stepping carefully over smashed debris and people obviously not so lucky as us I forced myself through the gaping hole where the window used to be. There was complete chaos outside as daylight filtered through the trees giving the whole scene an eerie appearance. The strong winds had obviously brought down a massive tree and left it straddling the railway line, we had hit the tree but we also found the object we had collided with, in the middle of all the carnage was the 'little fella'

Chapter 12.

Back Home Again.

It took sometime to help as many people as possible out of the carriages and onto the line. The wind was still howling wickedly and it was drizzling with rain. There was a real danger of another tree coming down and we had to get away from the crash site as quickly as we could. We were a bedraggled little mob that struggled off down the line towards Parkeston Quay. We had freed as many people as we could and had promised to get help for those still trapped. The whole thing was a nightmare and I couldn't help wondering how many people had lost their lives. It seemed an eternity before we came out of the trees and the fuel tanks of the oil refinery came into view. We slipped and tripped our way along the railway line finding it difficult to walk but eventually we met the first people we had seen since the crash and they helped us to the station and raised the alarm. Police and ambulance sirens soon filled the morning air and we were loaded into vehicles and transported to hospital for patching up. It wasn't until I had become a mass of bandages and been fully examined before being told I could go home that I discovered Ray had been brought into the hospital. He was more seriously injured than I was and the hospital staff said they would be keeping him in for a couple of days. He gave me his car keys and I promised to call and see Betty, she would want to visit him and I could bring her in his car. We tried to find out if anyone had been killed but there was little information available at the moment. News would be filtering through about the accident by now and I needed to contact Vicky to tell her I was alright. A police car took me and two other men back to Parkeston Quay Station as all the ambulances were still busy transporting people to hospital. Picking up Ray's car I took a couple of passengers who lived in Dovercourt and set off home. First it was a quick call at Ray's house to pick up Betty after assuring her that Ray was going to be alright and then on to mine with Betty in the car to reassure Vicky and her mother that I was not badly hurt. Vicky cried when she saw me and I realised I must have looked quite a sight covered in bandages, my clothes all filthy dirty and wet and she insisted that I had a quick change of clothes before leaving for the hospital with Betty and this at least made me feel a lot better. Ray had sustained a broken arm and internal injuries but the hospital assured us his injuries were not life threatening and he would be kept in under observation overnight and would probably be allowed home tomorrow. I left Betty at his bedside promising to pick her up later and returned home to see Vicky, her mother and Ashley.

I was beginning to feel very tired and was probably still suffering from shock so I had to drive very carefully. The weather was still terrible with gale force winds and driving rain and as I closed my front door I whispered a silent prayer of thanks that I had survived the accident. A strong cup of coffee and a piece of mother-in-laws fruit cake and I felt a lot better. Vicky wouldn't leave me alone fussing over me continually, asking if I had any pain and holding my hand and refusing to let it go. 'You're never going back to London to work' she insisted crying with relief, 'We might need the money but you're more important, I want you to take a job here.' 'Alright' I consoled her, 'There's plenty of time to talk about that ' I replied but at that moment I felt she was probably right. After a long rest I returned to the hospital with Vicky in Ray's car to collect Betty and bring her home. Vicky had refused to let me go alone and her mother said she would look after Ashley. Ray had come round and was his old self again which certainly cheered us up. I promised to pick him up tomorrow and we took Betty back to ours for the evening and watched television which was full of news of the accident. The pictures looked frightening but there had apparently been no loss of life although several passengers were in hospital with life threatening injuries. 'Will you go back to work at Collins?' Betty asked, 'I don't think so' I replied 'I don't want to spend so much time away from my family' 'If he does' Vicky answered 'He may not have any family to come back to.' I had to admit staying in Bristol had been a bit of an ordeal that I desperately wanted to forget, I must never let anything like that happen again, I was deeply in love with my wife and money or no money we would manage. By taking a job in Dovercourt I was not likely to allow a similar situation to arise and it would be nice to be home earlier in the evening to be with my family. So it was that I applied for a number of jobs in the local area and was finally accepted for one as a salesman in an electrical shop in Dovercourt High Street. It was a typical nine till five type of job and the pay was not very good but the breakfasts were considerably cheaper and there was very little travel. Added to that, I had got myself a little car which enabled me to take Vicky, her mum and Ashley out on Sundays.

Ray decided to sell his house and move to London in order to keep his job there and we miss their friendship, however since the accident we have made other friends and life goes on.

Besides his first love of short story writing
Len Biddlecombe is an accomplished poet.

In 2014 Len published 'Life of Love' his
personal tribute to his beloved wife Barbara.
It recorded his undying devotion to her
throughout their long married life.
He was interviewed on Radio TV and across
the internet for this volume and received
may congratulations and compliments.

Certainly as a testament to a man's love for
a woman there can be no finer tribute.
Check it out here

http://amzn.to/2oMhIIv

2015 saw the publication of 'Love of Life'
another collection of Len's poetry
Which explores his dramatically observant
reviews and thoughts on a long and happy
life.

http://amzn.to/2qeS5R3

Click these links to enable a free sampling
of Len's work.

Lightning Source UK Ltd.
Milton Keynes UK
UKOW01f1018200617

303734UK00001B/2/P